Look what people are saying about these talented authors!

Of Rhonda Nelson...

"I loved *The Keeper.* Jack and Mariette strike sparks off one another from their very first meeting and there is an emotional intensity to the mystery that will bring a few tears to your eyes."
—*Fresh Fiction*

"This highly romantic tale is filled with emotion and wonderful characters. It's a heart-melting romance."
—*RT Book Reviews* on *LETTERS FROM HOME*

"Wonderfully written and heart-stirring, the story flies by to the deeply satisfying ending."
—*RT Book Reviews* on *THE SOLDIER*

Of Karen Foley...

"[G]uaranteed to keep you turning the pages!"
—*RT Book Reviews* on *DEVIL IN DRESS BLUES*

"[T]he romance is intense and sure to please."
—*RT Book Reviews* on *HOT-BLOODED*

"With its blaze of heat, this is one very captivating tale!"
—*Cataromance Reviews* on *ABLE-BODIED*

ABOUT THE AUTHORS

A Waldenbooks bestselling author, two-time RITA® Award nominee, *RT Book Reviews* Reviewers Choice nominee and National Readers' Choice Award winner, **Rhonda Nelson** writes hot romantic comedy for the Harlequin Blaze line and other Harlequin Books imprints. With more than thirty-five published books to her credit, she's thrilled with her career and enjoys dreaming up her characters and manipulating the worlds they live in. She and her family make their chaotic but happy home in a small town in northern Alabama. She loves to hear from her readers, so be sure and check her out at www.readRhondaNelson.com, follow her on Twitter @RhondaRNelson and like her on Facebook.

Karen Foley is an incurable romantic. When she's not working for the Department of Defense, she's writing sexy romances with strong heroes and happy endings. She lives in Massachusetts with her husband and two daughters, an overgrown puppy and two very spoiled cats. Karen enjoys hearing from her readers. You can find out more about her by visiting www.karenefoley.com.

Rhonda Nelson
Karen Foley

BLAZING BEDTIME STORIES, VOLUME IX

ISBN-13: 978-0-373-79715-8

Recycling programs for this product may not exist in your area.

BLAZING BEDTIME STORIES, VOLUME IX

This edition published by arrangement with Harlequin Books S.A.

For questions and comments about the quality of this book please contact us at CustomerService@Harlequin.com.

www.Harlequin.com

Printed in U.S.A.

CONTENTS

THE EQUALIZER 7
Rhonda Nelson

GOD'S GIFT TO WOMEN 113
Karen Foley

RHONDA NELSON

THE EQUALIZER

For Cara Summers, a wonderful storyteller,
intrepid white-water kayaker—
I'm sure you remember Reno :-)—and all around
sweetheart. You're an inspiration, truly.

1

WITH A NAME SIMILAR TO A fabled outlaw, a passion for archery and a best friend named John Little, former Ranger Robin Sherwood had been the butt of many jokes, the bulk of which he'd accepted good-naturedly.

This, however, was different, because the situation he presently found himself in was a hell of his own making.

The maître d's eyes rounded in alarm, presumably because Robin was in every possible violation of the dress code and, while it *was* October, it wasn't yet quite Halloween. The conundrum had clearly flummoxed him.

"My usual table, please, Branson," Robin instructed briskly, sparing the man their usual chit-chat.

"Certainly, sir." His gaze slid over him once again—further confirmation that his eyes hadn't deceived him, Robin imagined—and, with a small gulp, Branson turned and led the way. "If you'll follow me."

"It's like Christmas has come early," John crowed behind him through fits of smothered, wheezing laughter. "And this is the best present *ever.*"

Determined to see this humiliation through to the end, Robin released a long suffering sigh and soldiered on.

A series of gasps, snickers and the clatter of fumbled cutlery followed him through the five-star restaurant. Though he was generally shameless and couldn't be bothered to care what people thought, he came as close to blushing as he ever hoped to and knew a small measure of relief when they finally arrived at their table.

"Paybacks are hell," Robin told him, his tone mild. He casually placed his napkin over his lap. "Just remember that."

John, irritatingly, continued to beam. He was in custom Armani, naturally—nothing off the rack would fit his Hercules-like frame—and every blond hair had been gelled meticulously into place. "You shouldn't have accepted the bet if you weren't certain of the outcome. Isn't that what you've always told me? A glass of Cristal," he happily told the waiter. "I'm celebrating."

Robin ordered a nice red wine and pretended not to notice that almost every eye in the exclusive restaurant was trained on him. He glanced out the window and admired the view instead. Downtown Atlanta lay spread out in a sea of night, punctuated with glittering lights and the occasional flash of neon. Though many of the storefronts were decorated with pretty mums, hay bales and gourds, fall seemed reluctant to make an official appearance thus far. It was unseasonably warm in Hotlanta for this time of year, which made his current outfit all the more uncomfortable. He grimaced.

That would teach him to bet when drunk.

"You look positively miserable," John said, smiling.

Robin smothered a curse and glared at his friend. "I'm hot."

"I imagine so." John's gaze darted to the top of Robin's head and he heaved a grudging sigh. "You can take off the hat, I suppose, but be careful not the crush that feather," he warned with a scowl. "It's rented, not bought."

Thank God for small favors, Robin thought. Better that the damned thing was returned than put away for future use. Particularly his. And given how much fun his friend was currently enjoying at his expense, he could easily see John pulling this little number out again and again.

Robin's phone suddenly vibrated in the leather pouch attached to his waist and, though it was bad form to answer it in the restaurant, he couldn't dismiss the call. It was an old friend from boarding school, Brian Payne, and more recently—more importantly—his new boss at Ranger Security. After the hit to his leg in Mosul had shredded his thigh muscle and thus ended his career in the military—as he'd envisioned it, anyway—Robin was eternally thankful for the job. Though there were many who would argue that he didn't need gainful employment, he'd never felt that way. Trust fund or not, he'd always needed a purpose. Needed to be useful. What was that old saying? Idle hands were the devil's playground?

He didn't know if he completely agreed with that—a battlefield seemed more apt—but he understood the sentiment. Busy people didn't have time to get into trouble. The only reason he'd been horsing around with John and had lost this damned bet was because he was between jobs at Ranger Security.

"Sherwood," he answered, turning away from the din.

"My Facebook feed just blew up with pictures of you, taken at Dolce Maria's, in what appears to be some sort of costume," Payne said, the humor barely registering in his cool voice. "I know it's been a while since you've been in polite society, Robin, but surely you haven't forgotten all the rules."

Robin swore hotly under his breath and Payne's chuckle echoed over the line.

"'The boy who wouldn't grow up,' one caption reads," Payne continued. He laughed appreciatively. "Clever."

Robin felt his eyes widen and he shot a dark look at John. "I'm not freakin' Peter Pan," he told him, outraged. "I'm Robin Hood, dammit." He glared accusingly across the table and lowered his voice. "I told you I needed the bow and arrows, but would you listen? No."

John blinked innocently. "I was afraid they'd call security if you came in with a weapon."

The staff would make them leave, more likely, thus ruining John's prank, Robin thought. Bastard.

"Ah, I see it now," Payne remarked, as though he'd just noticed something in the photo he'd missed before. He paused. "Fine. I'll ask the obvious question. *Why* are you dressed up like Robin Hood?"

Robin chewed the inside of his cheek for a moment before responding. "Because I lost a bet."

Payne grunted knowingly, as if this explanation made perfect sense. Which it did, Robin knew, because like him, Payne was a man who believed reneging on a bet—no matter how ill-conceived or asinine—was the same as lying.

He'd agreed to the terms and given his word. Balking was out of the question.

"And what if you hadn't lost?"

Robin grinned and glanced across the table at his completely unrepentant friend. "Then John would be dressed up like a vampire, acting out the *Twilight* saga via interpretative dance outside the High Museum. For tips."

Payne laughed softly again. "Oh, I would have liked to see that," he said. "Too bad you lost."

"There's always tomorrow," Robin told him, firmly in the glass-half-full camp. He took another sip of his wine. "Did you need anything else? Any new assignments come in?"

"No, that was all. Everything's covered for the moment. Enjoy the downtime. I'm sure it won't last."

Robin certainly hoped not. Though he had plenty to do to oversee his own business—look at financial reports, review his various charitable endeavors—he'd hired good people to attend to those things in his absence while in the military and, though he'd had a career change, he didn't mean to impose one on them, as well. That was not how one repaid good service.

In fact, everything he'd learned about being a good boss had come from following his father's short-lived example and by not taking any advice from his grandfather—railroad mogul, Henry Sherwood—who was a notoriously hard man. Robin inwardly snorted.

Hard hell. He was greedy and mean, a textbook narcissist whose first love was himself, his second, money. The old adage "only the good die young" had certainly proved true in Robin's experience. He imagined his grandfather would outlive Methuselah.

Currently, the old bastard was confined to his bed, a rotation of nurses on staff to see to his every need. His master suite had been outfitted to look like something that would no doubt rival NASA's Mission Command center, with banks of televisions streaming information from all over the globe—and the house and grounds, of course—attached to the walls and portable computers a mere roller table away at all times. He was just as formidable at eighty as he'd been at forty-eight and kept an eagle eye on his vast business and estate domains.

Though he'd always accused Robin of "being weak just like his father" and had never shown any interest in his grandson, evidently the significance of his own mortality had finally surfaced. Now the old man was acting as if he'd like nothing better than to groom Robin to take over the reins. Robin's response? Not no, but hell, no. He didn't have to own a crystal ball or possess any supernatural powers to know that they'd never see eye to eye, particularly when it came to how to treat employees. How the old man had managed to sire Robin's unbelievably kind father was an unsolvable mystery, one that had always baffled him.

Having lost his mother to an aneurysm while just a toddler, Robin had no memories of her, but he cherished the ones he had of his dad. And those were too few. Robin had been officially orphaned at fifteen, when his dad had died in a car accident. Gavin Sherwood had been buried less than a week before Robin's grandfather had shipped his grandson off to an exclusive boarding school—one notorious for corporal punishment, of course—in Maryland. That's where he'd met Payn, and a lifelong friendship was formed. Robin inwardly grinned. Nothing like a good thrashing to forge a bond.

As for John—his gaze darted to his friend across the table—that bond had been formed from the cradle. John Little was the son of Robin's father's best friend and as such, they'd grown up more like brothers than friends. Laughing one minute, pummeling the hell out of each other the next. Robin inwardly grinned. Good times.

John's father, Vince, had stepped in to fill the gap after his father had passed away and for that, Robin would always be thankful. Despite the distance once he'd been sent away to school, Vince and John had kept in constant contact, always writing and calling, occasionally visiting. And it was Vince who came to his graduation—both high school and college—and Vince who'd clapped him on the shoulder, tears in his eyes, and told him how proud his father would have been when he'd been accepted into Ranger school. It was Vince who shared memories of his dad, who'd painted a picture of him that he'd been able to hero-worship as a boy, and later appreciate as a man. A priceless gift, indeed.

Still thoroughly enjoying himself, John waved at a table of friends across the room and continued to savor his victory champagne. He sighed deeply. “Other than sex, there is absolutely nothing I like better than winning.”

“And since you do both so infrequently, I’m sure this is a novel experience for you,” Robin drawled.

John merely laughed and his gaze drifted fleetingly past Robin’s shoulder before finding his again. “Smart-assed bastard,” he groused good-naturedly. “I’m entitled to gloat. That’s what happens when you *win*.” He snorted. “You should know, you’ve done it often enough. By the way, have you been by the clinic to see Marion or are you still avoiding her?” he asked suddenly, his tone light.

Tone aside, the question itself carried enough weight to flatten an anvil and John bloody well knew it.

The clinic in question was the Michael Cross Clinic, one that Robin had founded as soon as he’d inherited at twenty-two in memory of a dear childhood friend who’d died officially of sepsis, but more truthfully of being poor and not having health insurance. Michael’s family had lived on the estate grounds and worked for his grandfather. His mother was the cook, his father the head gardener. By all rights, as a capable employer, Robin’s grandfather should have offered them coverage, but he’d been too tight-fisted to provide it.

Michael’s younger sister, Marion—the mere thought of her made something in Robin’s chest shift and ache—ran the clinic. She was a former friend, a onetime lover and the only woman Robin could honestly say ever terrified him.

Though his grandfather hadn’t approved of the Cross children as proper playmates for him, that hadn’t kept the four of them—Robin, Michael, John and later, Marion, who couldn't bear to be left behind—from spending as much time together as possible. They'd built a tree house and forts in the forest around the estate, swum in the creek that cut through the woods. They'd invented their own type of Morse code with flashlights and had communicated late into the night. They'd caught lightning bugs, played hide-and-seek and I Spy. Though five years younger than the rest of them, Marion had been determined to keep up and though she occasionally got on her older brother's nerves, Robin never minded when she came along.

She'd been special, even then.

And the adult version of Marion was even more potent. She made him feel things he couldn't recognize much less name, stirred a longing, an ache, a *need* beyond the basest level of attraction.

Because he'd needed to do something to show her that first, he wasn't like his grandfather and second that he had genuinely cared for her brother, Robin had founded the clinic and then handed her the reins to run as she saw fit once she'd graduated from college. He'd run into her half a dozen times in the ten years since she'd officially opened the door to the clinic and each time, no matter how fleeting, was more powerful than the last. It wasn't enough to talk to her—he needed to see her. It wasn't enough to see her—he had to touch her. Even if it was the merest brush of his shoulder against hers, it electrified him. Though he'd been with countless women over the past ten years—and had been with others prior to her—that single ill-conceived night with Marion a decade ago was still somehow the most significant experience he'd ever had, and had become the measuring stick by which any other coupling was evaluated.

Ridiculous, he knew, but there it was.

He'd been back in town for nearly three months now

and, while he'd done on-site visits to the other charities and businesses he supported, he'd avoided going to the clinic.

Why? Because he knew what would happen when he saw her—what he'd feel—and he had enough self-preservation instincts to delay it as long as possible.

Though there'd always been an easy camaraderie between them before, the tension now was palpable. She deliberately kept her distance and made sure they were never alone. It was obvious that she regretted their night together—and to some degree, he did, too, because he'd never been able to forget it—and wanted to keep their relationship on a strictly professional level.

His consolation? He knew she still wanted him, as well. He could practically feel the desire humming off her, caught glimpses of it when she thought he wasn't looking. He never left that clinic without feeling emotionally drained and wound tighter than a three-day clock.

"I'm not avoiding her," Robin lied, annoyed that John had noticed. "I've been busy. She has everything in hand at the clinic. There's no reason for me to check up on her." There. That sounded perfectly logical. Even John should appreciate that.

"How about just checking in *on* her then?" John pressed, the dart penetrating. "She's a friend, isn't she? You've known her most of your life."

Robin scowled, growing increasingly uncomfortable with this topic of conversation. "I know how long I've known her, dammit," he snapped, reaching again for his glass. "I don't need you to tell me."

John shrugged, seemingly unconcerned, then leaned forward and smiled with all of his teeth. "Maybe so, but do you know what you *do* need me to tell you?"

John's gaze shifted past his shoulder once more and a prickling of uneasiness slid up Robin's spine as a grin that wasn't directed at him broke impossibly wider over his friend's face.

"What?" he asked ominously.

John beamed at him. "Marion's here and headed this way. Put the hat back on."

2

MARION CROSS HAD BEEN LOCKED in a state of dreadful anticipation since the moment she learned several months ago that Robin Sherwood was back in Atlanta. As her boss, she'd imagined their first meeting would take place at the clinic—rumor had it he'd been making the rounds, doing on-site inspections of his various interests around town, though irritatingly, he hadn't made it to hers yet. She didn't know whether to be relieved or insulted and, if she was honest, she'd admit to being a little hurt, as well. She hadn't expected to be the first on his list—too much history—but she'd expected him to at least make it.

Although, had anyone told her that she'd run into him at one of the city's finest, most exclusive restaurants dressed in an extravagant Robin Hood costume, she would have never believed it. Her lips quirked.

Of course, knowing Robin, she probably should have.

No doubt this was the result of one of his and John's equally notorious and ridiculous bets. They'd been doing it as long as she could remember. The daring and daunting, goading and gloating, the cork-brained testosterone-induced idiocy that, for reasons that would always escape her, she found reluctantly endearing. There was something so natural about their friendship, the mutual understanding of what made the other one tick. It was a beautiful thing to watch.

John immediately smiled and got to his feet when he saw her. His bright blue eyes twinkled with mischievous pleasure. "Marion," he said warmly, wrapping his massive arms around her. The only thing *little* about John was his last name. More blond Adonis than ogre, he'd left a string of broken hearts around Atlanta.

Unaccountably nervous, she returned the embrace. "Hi, John. It's good to see you."

He drew back. "You, too, sprite. You're looking lovely as always."

She murmured her thanks, her heartbeat suddenly thundering in her ears. She didn't have to see him to know that Robin was looming right behind her—she could *feel* him. The weight of his presence rolled over her, prickling her skin. Her stomach gave an involuntarily little jump and her pulse quickened right along with her mounting anxiety. She felt the weight of his gaze bore into the back of her head, then trail ever-so-slowly down her frame—lingering on her ass, of course—leaving a rash of gooseflesh in its wake.

She gulped and mentally braced herself.

It took every iota of willpower she possessed to turn around and face him.

Naturally, she still wasn't prepared. Her breath caught in her throat, her insides vibrated like a tuning fork and longing, stark and potent, rose so quickly she nearly wobbled on her feet.

That's what he did to her. What he'd always done to her, damn him.

In a just world, he would have looked utterly ridiculous in the costume. His powerful shoulders wouldn't have been displayed to mouthwatering advantage beneath the loose linen material, his chest emphasized by the leather vest, his narrow waist accentuated with the belt. The knee-high boots wouldn't have drawn attention to his muscled thighs and the distinct bulge that formed between them beneath the obscenely thin pants. Even the hat, curse him, perched at a jaunty angle on his head, looked good with his tawny curls and seemed to highlight the elegantly masculine lines of his face. Heavily lashed hazel eyes peered down at her with a mixture of rueful humor, a hint of trepidation and something else, something not readily identifiable.

It was that something else, naturally, that would haunt her.

He doffed his hat and offered her an extravagant, theatrical bow. "My lady," he said, his eyes twinkling.

She nodded primly, playing along, and arched a brow. "Going to a costume party later, or is this a new trend I'm unaware of?"

"Oh, it's definitely a new trend in men's fashion," he assured her, as though he were an expert on the subject. "It's all the rage in Paris, trust me. You can't go anywhere without seeing one of the Three Musketeers, Napoleon, Henry the Eighth or even Davy Crockett."

She chuckled. "Davy Crockett? Really?"

Humor lit his gaze. "It's the coonskin cap," he confided conspiratorially, leaning close enough to make her pulse clamor. "They can't get enough of it."

"It's getting a little deep in here, Robin, and you're the only one wearing boots," John interjected. He glanced at Marion. "The truth is Robin thought he could put an arrow through a tire swing from a hundred yards."

She didn't see why that should have posed any problem. He'd always been a keen archer. He'd been competing for as long as she could remember. Truth be told, she'd always enjoyed watching him shoot. The careful way his fingers nocked the arrow, the wide-legged stance, the way his muscles rippled in his long arms as he drew back the string, then sighted his target. Every motion was deliberate, but strangely natural, a beautiful combination of skill and strength. Just the thought of it made her belly flutter and grow warm.

With effort, she ignored the sensation and frowned. “That shouldn’t have—”

John grinned. “He was knee-walking drunk and the tire swing was in motion.”

Her gaze darted to Robin’s and she smothered a laugh. “And you’re surprised you lost?”

He sighed deeply. “*Chagrined,* I think, is the word you’re looking for,” he said, hanging his head in mock shame. “And for the record, I still hit the swing.”

“All things considered, that was damned impressive,” John admitted with a reflective nod. He looked at Marion, his expression hopeful. “Can you join us? We’d—”

She inwardly gasped and shook her head. “Sorry. I’m with a—”

“Ah, there you are,” her almost forgotten companion Jason said, sidling up next to her. He glanced at John and Robin—doing an understandable double take—and then slung an arm over her shoulder, which immediately set her teeth on edge. “I was beginning to wonder if I needed to send out a search party.”

Strictly speaking, this wasn’t a date, though she was sure Jason Reeves would beg to differ. Jason’s goal was to get her into bed—Marion’s goal was to collect the substantial pledge he’d made to the clinic two months ago. A recent newcomer to wealth through an innovative fast food chain, she knew that he had the money, but he didn’t seem to understand the definition of a pledge, that it truly was a commitment. When the repeated but polite reminders hadn't worked, she'd made a phone call—sometimes that's what it took, after all—and he'd taken the opportunity to invite her to dinner, promising to bring along his checkbook. This was their third dinner and she still hadn't seen the check he'd promised.

She'd learned an awful lot about him, though. Lots and lots and lots. Ad nauseum. In fact, she could safely say that *he* was his favorite topic of conversation. It was extremely unpleasant…but, unfortunately, necessary.

Though Robin's yearly donation for operations was substantial, there was always new equipment to be bought, newer, better medicines she needed to have on hand and more patients to be seen. It was the sad reality of the current economy and health care situation, one that never seemed to change from generation to generation. Her heart pricked.

She knew that all too well.

Marion had always prided herself on staying under budget, but by soliciting donations she'd managed to put enough in savings to float them for a while should they need it, as well as add additional staff, equipment, medicines and, ultimately, care for more patients. She had developed a good working relationship with the doctors and nurses who volunteered their time and she ran an extremely tight ship. Though her secretary, Justine, often accused her of having no life outside the clinic—one she couldn't confidently deny—Marion didn't care. The clinic and the people who came through it *were* her life, one that Robin had handed her when she'd graduated from college. It was one with purpose, one that met a true need in the community and one that honored her late brother.

Michael had only been sixteen when he'd died—she'd been eleven at the time—and there wasn't a day that went by when she didn't think of him, when she didn't miss his smile, when she didn't mourn the loss of the life he should have had.

Because they hadn't had health insurance, her parents had always been careful about what sort of illness or accident had warranted a trip to the doctor's office. Had Michael seen a doctor when his symptoms first started to show, there was no doubt in her mind that her brother would be alive today.

But he hadn't.

And by the time her parents had realized that Michael was in serious danger, it was too late. He'd died within hours of getting to an emergency room.

Though she'd always adored Robin and his father, Marion had never liked Henry Sherwood. After Michael died, she'd positively hated him. The father she'd loved and respected turned to drink and, within months of her brother's death, he'd abandoned the family. She hadn't heard from him in years. Her mother, left with little choice, had stayed on and continued to work for Mr. Sherwood, though she'd ultimately blamed his stinginess for the death of her son. She'd become bitter and distant, a mere shadow of the lively, hardworking woman Marion remembered.

Odd how a single occurrence could change the landscape of one's life. Michael's death had marked one period for Marion, taking over the clinic, the next. Her gaze swung to Robin and her heart gave a pathetic little jump. Intuition told her if she wasn't careful, Robin Sherwood's return to Atlanta could herald another era, one that would spell absolute disaster for her heart.

Though he'd never orbited around her universe very often or for very long, he'd never failed to make a substantial impact.

Most significantly, the night before she'd left for college and he'd left for the military. It was a new beginning for both of them, with all the excitement and anxiety that came along with them. Marion had thought a lot about that night over the years—he'd been her first, after all—and though she could easily chalk up what happened between them to too much alcohol, recklessness, hormones and nostalgia, ultimately she knew better. It had felt magical, fated even. She'd had the occasional partner since then, of course, but nothing ever came close to how Robin had made her feel. The desperation, the desire, the unadulterated *need.* She was drawn to him in a way that she'd never been to another person. She always had been.

When she'd first learned that he'd been wounded in Iraq, the panic and dread that had rocketed through her had sent her into the nearest chair, her head between her knees to keep from hyperventilating. The mere thought of him being hurt—or worse, a world that he was no longer in—had literally terrified her. It was even more proof, as if she needed it, that he was still, after all these years, the most significant man in her life.

Was it because he'd set the bar so high? Marion wondered now. Or was it something else? Were the feelings she had for him genuinely that special, not just a romanticized memory of what was?

No matter. Michael's death was always going to haunt them—the association with his grandfather and the part he'd played in her brother's death was a shadow they'd never be able to shake. And, though she knew enough dinner etiquette to get her through a nice meal, she'd just as soon eat a slice of pizza over a paper plate. Because rubbing elbows with the Atlanta's wealthy set was necessary to get additional funding for the clinic, she'd learned to speak a bit of the language and had acquired a decent second-hand wardrobe for formal events, but she never failed to feel like an imposter, an outsider in a world she didn't even want to be a part of.

Robin's world.

Granted, he'd never made her feel that way, but his grandfather had. The old man had never even bothered to learn her name, had simply called her Cook's Daughter. It was degrading.

Jason gave her shoulder a gentle squeeze. "Aren't you going to introduce me to your friends, Marion?"

She blinked, startled out of her reverie. "Er, yes, of course. This is Robin Sherwood and John Little," she said, gesturing to both in turn. "They're old friends of mine."

As though he were a shark and had caught the scent of blood in the water—but only if blood smelled like money—Jason's expression brightened with shrewd intensity. Clearly recognizing what businesses they belonged to—the truly wealthy was a small set, after all—he extended his hand. "Jason Reeves," he said smoothly with a painfully affected smile. She was surprised his eye tooth didn't sparkle. "It's a pleasure to meet you." He glanced at Robin. "Sherwood Holdings, am I correct?"

At Robin's nod, Jason flushed with giddy pleasure, then turned to John and arched a brow. "Red Rock Developments?" The massive development company was responsible for roughly half of all new construction in the greater Atlanta area.

John's jovial expression had devolved from blank to a bemused WTF. "That's right."

"Excellent," her non-date enthused, further mortifying her with his utter lack of self-awareness. "My family's in commercial eateries. We're new to the big business scene—we didn't build any railroads," he said aside to Robin with a wink, "but we've seen *substantial* growth and are rapidly expanding into other markets. It's an excellent time to be in the food business."

Marion would like to know when it was a bad time to be in the food business—everyone had to eat, after all—but rather than linger and allow this train wreck of a conversation to keep going, she pasted a bright smile on her face, glanced past Jason's shoulder and said, "Oh, I think they're ready to serve us. We should—" She attempted to nudge him away, but he held fast.

Evidently realizing that she was mortified and miserable, Robin decided that was the perfect time to ask Jason about his "commercial eateries." She inwardly snorted. *Newsflash, Jason. It's called "fast food."*

"Commercial eateries?" Robin asked, his tone thoughtful. "It sounds fascinating."

She couldn't believe he said that with a straight face. John turned and coughed into his arm.

"Oh, it is," Jason told him, utterly delighted. "It's—"

"Carnival Cuisine," Marion interjected quickly, hoping to shut down the long and involved story that led to his family's business. "Funnel cakes, corn dogs, candied apples, deep-fried Snickers, cotton candy," she said, the words practically running together, she said them so fast. "Anything you can get at a traditional carnival. Genius, right?"

To her horror, John's face lit up with genuine interest. "It is. I went through the drive-thru recently for an ear of roasted corn and a turkey leg. Good stuff." He jabbed Robin in the side. "Remember, I told you about it?

"I do remember," Robin said, watching her closely. Those hazel eyes were rife with knowing humor, his beautifully sculpted lips curled into an almost-smile. He was enjoying this entirely too much, the wretch.

"Another satisfied customer," Jason remarked with a

smug chuckle. "I knew it would be a success. I just knew it. I had faith in the idea—it was mine, after all," he bragged proudly, "and was certain that it would resonate with the masses."

Oh, good Lord, Marion thought with a massive internal eye-roll. What masses? They were in the South, for heaven's sake. Butter, lard and sugar were practically their own food groups. Good ones, too, in moderation she'd admit. Still…

Robin gestured widely to the table. "Have a seat and tell us all about it. I'd love to hear where you two met, as well. I'm sure that's equally interesting."

"It's not, really," Jason told him, plopping his rude ass into a chair without a thought for her. "It was at one of those tedious charity events. I'm sure you know the kind."

"I typically like those," the Prince of Mischief, as she'd renamed Robin, said. "It gives me a good feeling when I know my money is doing something important."

With another veiled glance at her, Robin chewed the inside of his cheek, then, ever the gentleman, pulled out a chair for her and quirked a brow. Seething, she accepted it grudgingly and mentally braced herself for further humiliation.

"Right, right. Me, too," Jason immediately backpedaled. "That's what I meant."

And that's how the rest of the meal went. Robin and John let Jason liberally share his opinions, then purposely voiced a different view—no matter how ludicrous—and watched him recant and agree with them.

It was a game. They kept score. Occasionally, she'd referee.

By the end of the evening, Jason had renounced real butter in favor of margarine, switched political parties, promised to cancel his country club membership and name his firstborn son Sue because Johnny Cash had a point. (Yes, he did, but that wasn't it!) To her disbelief, Jason had whipped out his cell phone and downloaded the Man in Black's "A Boy Named Sue," and set it as his new ringtone. At John's urging, he'd purchased the accompanying screen saver.

It was at that point that Marion started to drink.

And despite the fact that she'd arrived with Jason—who still hadn't given her the damned check for the clinic—it was Robin, naturally, who ended up driving her home. A smarter woman would have protested, but her foolish heart had lifted at the thought and a secret thrill of anticipation had whipped through her. She inwardly sighed.

Which only served to prove how little perspective she had when it came to Robin Sherwood. And the hell of it? Right now, she didn't care.

3

ROBIN WAITED UNTIL the automatic door locks had clicked into place before sending Marion a sidelong glance. "Your boyfriend is charming," he remarked as he aimed the truck toward her address. "Eager. Hungry." Self-important. Small-minded. A prick, Robin thought silently. In what sort of world did a girl like Marion go out with a guy like him? Honestly, when he'd watched Jason's arm go around her shoulders, Robin's irritation level had needled dangerously toward Kick His Ass.

Marion sighed, a weary smile playing over her lips. "He's not my boyfriend."

Irrational relief wilted through him. "Has anyone told him that? Because he seems to be laboring under the assumption that the two of you are an item."

She gave an indelicate snort. "Jason labors under a lot of incorrect assumptions. Or hadn't you noticed?" she asked, sending him a pointed glance.

Even in the darkened interior, he could see the knowing humor glinting in her ice-blue eyes. They were remarkable, those eyes. The purest, brightest blue, very round with an exotic lift in the far corners that gave her an almost catlike appearance. Paired with that milky fair skin and gleaming black hair, she put him in mind of John William Waterhouse's painting of Pandora opening the box. The metaphor wasn't lost on him, but it hadn't kept him from buying the print or hanging it in his living room, either.

Marion had the same grace, an innate regality that would put some of the world's modern-day royalty to shame. She was strikingly lovely, beautiful to watch and, refreshingly, not the least bit aware of it.

"He certainly has a lot of opinions," Robin conceded. "And is more than willing to share them."

"Or change them, when properly led," she remarked drolly. "You and John were in fine form tonight."

Yes, they were, he thought, inwardly smiling. But when presented with such an easy target, how were they to resist? "It's the costume," Robin confided. "It brings out the worst in me."

He felt her gaze skim over him, an infinitesimal pause along his thigh. A gratifying flush of color bloomed beneath her skin and she swallowed, drawing his attention to the fine muscles of her throat. She released a shaky breath. "I don't think it's fair to blame the costume for that."

"You're right," he said. "It's John, but we've been friends too long now to change the status quo."

She chuckled, the sound low and smoky between them. "I don't think it's fair to blame John, either."

He negotiated a turn. "Well, we have to blame someone, otherwise I'd have to assume that you thought it was some sort of character flaw on my part, and—" he sighed deeply and gave his head a lamentable shake "—that just wouldn't do."

Another soft laugh. "Oh, because you care what I think?"

He flashed a grin at her. "Of course."

She hummed under her breath, studying him for a moment. It was unnerving, that measured stare. It made him feel exposed, laid bare and open. Vulnerable. "You've gotten better at it," she said.

Shaken, Robin attempted to shrug the odd sensation off. "I'm always trying to improve, so that's not surprising, but what exactly have I gotten better at?"

"Bullshit," she told him. "You're a black belt."

A bark of laughter erupted from his throat. "A black belt in bullshit? Really? And here I thought I was being charming," he drawled.

"That, too," she admitted, seemingly reluctantly. "But it doesn't make you any less a pain in the ass." She sat a little straighter and shot him an accusing glare. "You insisted that we sit with you simply for the sport of it—just so Jason could double as the entertainment. And you've no doubt cost me another evening I'll never get back with Mr. I-Love-Myself-Enough-For-Both-of-Us. Awesome," she said, her voice loaded with sarcasm. "That's just what I wanted."

"I'm…sorry," Robin said, because an apology seemed like an appropriate response to that interesting but thoroughly nonsensical diatribe. Another evening that she'll never get back? What the hell was she talking about? Hadn't she been on a date?

She grunted. "Ha. No, you're not."

He wasn't, really, but there was no way she could be certain of that. He'd forgotten what a know-it-all she could be. How odd that he hated the quality in others, but found it endearing when it came to her.

"You're smiling," she said, as though she'd read his mind. "Interestingly enough, it makes one doubt your sincerity."

His grin widened. "Sorry."

Her ripe lips twitched, taking the sting out of her outrage. "This is my street."

He glanced at his GPS. The unit, or "Hilda," who'd been giving him turn by turn instructions, hadn't said a word.

She arched a wry brow and bit the corner of her lip. "I'll admit I've had a little too much to drink, but I'm not so far gone that I don't know where I live."

He made the turn, and Hilda immediately found her voice. "Recalculating."

The put-upon announcement garnered a chuckle from the passenger seat.

"How civil," she remarked.

"Ha," he told her. "That's just its polite way of saying, 'You're going the wrong way, fool.'"

"Third house on the right, fool," she said with an affected Swedish accent, much like Hilda's.

He grinned and pulled into her narrow driveway, admittedly curious about her lair. You could tell a lot about a person by looking at the things they surrounded themselves with. Color, texture, art, knickknacks and keepsakes. A home was the sum total of a personality, told in objects, shared in photos.

Though nice and in a decent part of town—one the city had decided to revitalize—her house was much more modest than he would have thought, particularly given her salary. He knew it, after all, since it was part of the budget for the clinic, and it had always been important to him that she was well compensated for her work. It was hard, he knew, not to mention important and emotionally draining. Rewarding, too, he imagined, but rewards didn't pay the bills.

A traditional shotgun style, the house was pink, a color that clearly said "No Men Allowed," because no self-respecting man would live in a pink house. Interesting. He filed it away for future thought. Lacy white fretwork decorated the small front porch, giving it a whimsical appeal. Potted yellow mums and some sort of purple flowers marched along both sides of the steps and, though it was dark, he could make out a bird bath nestled in the shrubbery. All in all, very charming, very efficient. Much like its owner.

She unfastened her seat belt and dug around her purse for her keys, then turned to look at him. He knew that particular look, though admittedly he wasn't used to seeing it directed at him. "Thanks so much for—"

"Hold that thought," Robin told her before she could give him the official brush-off. He jumped out of the truck, bustled around the front and then opened her door for her.

"—bringing me home," she finished, looking mildly startled. She swallowed, the long, creamy column of her throat moving with the effort. "You don't have to walk me in. I don't want to put you to any more trouble."

Wrong. He unnerved her every bit as much as she unnerved him, but he was too damned curious about her—what had made her the person she was today, specifically—to allow her to send him packing now. A pink house? Really? Had it been pink when she'd bought it or had she painted it this anti-man color on purpose? And why was she going to have to go out with Jason again? What was she doing out with him in the first place? Especially if she didn't consider him—thank God—dating material?

The answers to these questions were tucked away in that intriguing little mind of hers and, if he could spend a bit of time with her, he hoped to coax them right out of that beautiful, kissable mouth.

This was why he'd avoided her. He was never curious enough to care about any other woman. Only her.

"It's no trouble at all," he said, offering her his hand to help her out the passenger side, another mistake, but one he couldn't seem to help. She hesitated only the merest fraction of a second, but his gut clenched all the same. Then her small palm connected with his—soft silky skin, delicate feminine bones—and a jolt of sensation rocketed through him, an odd mixture of relief, longing, anticipation and desire. His dick instantly stirred beneath the thin fabric of his breeches, as though his skin somehow recognized hers.

Her chest rose in an inaudible gasp and she glanced up, her gaze meeting his. Silent confirmation that she'd felt it, too. "Th-thank you," she murmured. She stood and quickly released his hand.

Robin closed the door and followed her up the walkway. A slight breeze lifted the ends of her hair and molded the garnet-colored dress she wore even more closely to her frame. The dress was long with bell-like sleeves, and a small, jeweled sash encircled her slim waist, then tied and dangled over her hip. He mentally added a halo of flowers on her head. She might as well have stepped out of one of those Waterhouse paintings.

Which was fitting, he supposed, because she certainly had the renaissance frame to pull off the look. She was tall and slender, but generously curved and lush in all the right places. No doubt the hips she probably thought were too wide were the very ones he'd like to hold on to while he plunged in and out of her warm, soft body. A natural cradle made for carnal things. A vision of her arching up beneath him temporarily blinded him, making him stumble on the path, and he uttered a low curse, painfully aroused and mortified.

Especially since there was no room for error in these damned pants.

Marion paused at the door, then turned to face him. The send-him-packing look was firmly back in place and it galled him to no end. He wasn't some random guy she'd just met—she'd known him nearly all her life. Manners alone should dictate a cup of coffee, at the very least. A slice of cake, if it was on hand. Granted, he'd been in the military a long time, but he still knew enough about Southern hospitality to know that.

"Thanks again for the ride," she said, her skin especially creamy beneath the glow of her porch light. If she wore any lipstick at all, it had long ago worn off, leaving her mouth a lovely rose color. "Can I expect you at the clinic anytime soon?" she asked lightly. Too lightly.

"First thing in the morning," he said, just to unnerve her. "Things are slow at Ranger Security at the moment. Do you mind if I use your bathroom before I leave?" he asked. "It's a bit of a drive to Hawthorne Lake."

Her eyes rounded in surprise, from his request or the Hawthorne Lake comment, he couldn't be sure. "Er, yes, of course." Her shoulders sagged minimally—a sign of defeat?—and she inserted the key into the lock and opened the door. A loud meow immediately issued from the depths of the house and then a very large gray cat with misshapen ears streaked straight at Marion and curled around her legs.

Meow, *meow,* MEOW.

She chuckled, set her purse aside and then scooped the massive animal up into her arms and cuddled it close. "Yes, yes, I know. I'm late again. My apologies, Angus." She glanced at Robin, a smile on her face. "The bathroom's through there," she said, gesturing through the dining room door.

He nodded and headed in that direction, taking note of the wide plank hardwood floors, the squashy floral patterned furniture arranged around the working fireplace. Soft pastels covered the walls—pale pink in the living room, robin's-egg-blue in the dining room, pale yellow in the kitchen and, since the bathroom had been added by erecting another wall along the back of the kitchen to create a small hall, a quick peek into her bedroom revealed a lilac shade with spindly white furniture and mountains of accent pillows.

The whole place was light and airy and, more significantly...*girly.*

She might as well put a sign out by the curb that said No Boys Allowed.

He'd noted several pictures of her family—mostly Michael—on her mantle, a collection of old colored-glass bottles and several prints from the Art Deco era—Parrish, Fox, Icart. A corkboard with postcards of various famous landscapes—Venice, Rome, Paris, Greece, London—was adhered to the wall in the kitchen, along with the caption "Bucket List." Another little insight into her soul.

"Can I get you something to drink?" she called, much to his delight. "Coffee? Iced tea?"

"Iced tea would be great," he said. He hadn't really needed to use the restroom, of course. It had just been a ploy to get inside. She probably suspected that, so he flushed the commode and washed his hands just in case she was listening.

She was just sliding a few cookies onto a plate when he entered the kitchen. Spying the dessert, his eyes widened and a hopeful smile slide over his lips. "Are those—"

"Snickerdoodles?" she finished, shooting him a grin. "Yes, they are. It's my mother's recipe and still my favorite, though I still haven't managed to make them quite as well as she did."

If his childhood could be labeled with flavors, no doubt butter, brown sugar and cinnamon would be high on the list. The cookies were melt-in-your-mouth delicious. He swallowed, his smile dimming. The cookies had been

Michael's favorite, as well. Marion's mother had stopped making them after he'd died and no amount of hints or wheedling had changed her mind.

A quick glance at Marion's face confirmed that she knew he'd made the connection, that he remembered. She released a small breath and handed him a glass of tea. "Let's go to the living room, shall we?" *And get this over with* hung, unspoken, between them.

Back to square one, Robin thought with an inward sigh. And it was too damned familiar.

4

FEELING AN INCREASING SENSE of doom, Marion led the way to the living room and watched Robin lower his considerable frame onto her ultrafeminine couch. He should have looked out of place—ridiculous even, considering that costume—and yet…he didn't.

Just as she'd feared.

Marion had bought the house a little more than three years ago and had personally overseen every nuance of the renovation. It was the first time she'd ever had a place of her own. Before that, she'd lived with her mother. Guilt could be a serious tether.

When her mother had decided to move to North Carolina to live with her sister, Marion had taken the opportunity to finally feather her own nest. Friends kept trying to convince her to get a bigger place, one that would accommodate a future husband and family, but Marion had ignored their advice because she wanted something that was just *hers*. Did that mean she was opposed to this mythical husband and family? No, though admittedly she was beginning to have her doubts as to whether or not either of those were in her future. It just meant that she wasn't going to live in perpetual expectation of that happening. Her gaze slid to Robin and her heart gave a little squeeze.

He was the first man, other than the ones she'd hired to renovate, who'd stepped over her threshold. She could only name two who'd ever made it to the front porch. No doubt he thought she was being ungrateful and rude by not inviting him in, but the truth of the matter was, she'd wanted to issue the invitation too much.

Robin Sherwood was her Achilles' heel, her ultimate weakness. She knew that an inside visit would shatter the boundaries she'd been so carefully trying to put into place. Of course, the fissure had started tonight when she'd seen him again. It was easy to imagine that she had some sort of control over her feelings when he wasn't around.

And now he was going to be around—in Atlanta—on a permanent basis.

At Hawthorne Lake.

"When did you move to Hawthorne Lake?" she asked, unable to help herself. It had never occurred to her that he wasn't living on the family estate. Though she hadn't seen him in years—not since she'd moved her mother out of their old cottage—she knew his grandfather was in terrible health. Not that she cared, of course. He was a rotten man—it was only fitting that he…rot. Which was horrible, she knew, particularly coming from her, but Marion couldn't help the way she felt. Henry Sherwood was an awful, awful man, the one who was ultimately responsible for the death of her brother. Forgiveness—and perspective, she'd admit—was never going to be forthcoming.

"I've always lived there when I was stateside," he said. "Because Ranger Security is downtown, I considered a loft, but decided I'd rather make the commute than live with the noise." He smiled at her, his honey-colored eyes crinkling at the corners. "Cottonwood is peaceful. I like watching the sunset over the meadow, listening to the bullfrogs croak from the pond."

He couldn't have surprised her more if he'd told her he lived in a mud-covered hut. Cottonwood was an old two-story white clapboard farmhouse that was idyllic but not grand. It sat back on a small knoll overlooking a pond and was surrounded by a grove of cottonwood trees, thus its name. It achieved a bit of notoriety during the Civil War, when Robert E. Lee was purported to have stayed there. Her mother had taken them all there the summer before Michael died, during Robin, John and Michael's "civil war phase."

They'd tromped over a lot of battlefields and visited several plantation homes, but Cottonwood had appealed to Marion the most because of the second-story porch. At the time it had felt a bit like a tower and she'd been going through her princess stage. Unbeknownst to the rest of them, she'd slipped away from the tour, ducked under the velvet rope and snuck up there. Michael ultimately spotted her from the ground and demanded that she come down—which she'd refused to do of course because "he wasn't the boss of her"—and it had been Robin who'd coaxed her back. He'd told her that princesses weren't meant to be locked away in musty old towers, they were supposed to be at Court. That had made sense to her, so she'd come down of her own volition. She smiled, remembering.

At any rate, it was a lovely house, one that held a special memory in her heart and it would definitely accommodate a sizable family.

The thought was oddly depressing.

She cleared her throat. "I imagine it would be."

He arched a brow, an odd expression in his eyes. Hopeful? "You remember it then?"

She nodded, offered him a grin. "I do."

"You should come see it sometime," Robin said, gifting her with another of those charming smiles. "I'll give you the whole tour, even show you the room Lee supposedly slept in." His gaze turned mischievous. "I'll even give you unlimited access to the second-story porch."

Of course he would remember. Something told her Robin Sherwood didn't forget much. Still…

Marion made a noncommittal sound and popped another bite of cookie in her mouth. Temping though it was, she didn't think so. She was too damned aware of him now—the slope of his jaw, the exact curve of his lips, the masculine veins in his large hands, the muscles bunching beneath the fabric of his costume every time he moved, not to mention the tawny curls hugging the shell of his ear. Something about those irreverent curls against the strangely vulnerable skin around his ear, his neck, made her long to nuzzle them with her nose, to breathe him in. Her nipples tightened behind her bra and a ribbon of heat unfurled low in her belly. She felt herself leaning toward him, inexplicably drawn to him.

As always.

With effort, she righted herself.

Robin shot her a speculative glance, one that made her worry that he knew the effect he had on her, that he knew exactly how she felt about him. Every wicked, depraved thought.

"So if Jason wasn't a date, then what were you doing with him?"

Back to that, were they? She released an exasperated sigh. "Trying to collect a pledge he made to the clinic. He keeps 'forgetting' to bring his checkbook."

Robin frowned and his gaze sharpened. "I wasn't aware that you were soliciting pledges."

She knew he wasn't. Because she hadn't told him.

Thankfully, she'd prepared for this conversation, had been in anticipation of it for three long months. Marion lifted an unconcerned shoulder and feigned an irreverence she didn't feel. "It's common practice with non-profit organizations."

He set his glass aside and she felt the full force of his regard. "I realize that, but when did we start doing it?"

"Two years ago." She took another nibble of cookie. "We had a big kick-off. It was a huge success. I was able to purchase a new X-ray machine with the proceeds."

He made a noise low in his throat, but she couldn't tell if that was a good thing or a bad thing. He was unnaturally still, as though he were holding himself that way on purpose. Probably to keep from throttling her, Marion imagined.

"Marion, if you needed more money, then why didn't you just ask for it? You know I would have approved whatever you—"

"The budget is more than generous, Robin," she said. "And I know that I'm fortunate in that regard. But surely you realize that if I can raise the money to buy the equipment and medicines to treat more people, then I'm going to do it. I didn't expect a budget increase and I didn't start doing this in order to angle for one—that's precisely why I didn't tell you—but I would be remiss if I didn't pursue all avenues of funding available to us. It's part of my job to solicit donations." She grimaced and heaved a sigh. "Granted, there are some people who are more difficult to deal with than others—like Jason, for instance—but for the most part, people around here are glad to be a part of what we're doing." She paused. "I'm proud of that…and I think you should be, too."

"Of course, I am," he said, his gaze still annoyingly inscrutable. "I just wish you'd mentioned it to me sooner. I would have been more than happy to help. Get donations," he added quickly. "Or amend your budget. Whatever would have made you happy."

It had been so long since someone had considered her happiness that the comment took her aback and left her feeling shaken and out of sorts. Thankfully, Robin looked as startled by the comment as she felt. For one heart-stoppingly agonizing instant, she couldn't rip her gaze away from his, couldn't unsee the turmoil roiling in those amazing hazel eyes.

"I knew you'd understand," she murmured, for lack of anything better.

Abruptly, he stood. "I'd like a list, please."

Marion blinked and found her feet as well, then followed him to the door. "A list? A list of what?"

"Of the people who currently have outstanding pledges."

She winced. "That's a long list."

He flashed an unconcerned smile. "In the meantime, I'll start with Jason."

Her stupid heart did a giddy somersault and she chuckled at the low growl she heard in his voice. "You don't have to do this, you know."

"I know. But I want to." His gaze softened, traced every facet of her face and lingered hungrily on her mouth. He bent forward and brushed a kiss against her cheek. His lips were warm and soft and his scent curled around her, something dark and woodsy. Sinful. "Good night, Marion. See you in the morning."

She smothered a whimper, willing her trembling, traitorous body to still, and let go a small, resigned breath. Like it or not, for better or for worse, Robin Sherwood was back in her life again. It was only a matter of time before he was back in her heart—assuming that he'd ever left, which was doubtful—and back in her bed, as well.

Heaven help her.

"Good night, Robin."

THE INTOXICATING SCENT OF HER skin still in his nostrils, Robin descended the front steps and made the short walk to his car, more irritated, exhilarated and turned on than he'd ever been in his life.

The rational part of his brain understood that Marion was right—soliciting donations was perfectly within the scope of her duties as managing director at the clinic. Unfortunately, the other side of his brain—the one that felt like she'd lopped his balls off—was having difficulty understanding why she hadn't come to him for help. Had he ever refused her anything for the clinic? Had he ever given her any indication that her work there wasn't important to him?

No, dammit, he hadn't.

He would have given her further funding, would have bought the equipment, medicines, hired additional staff, if needed. As he'd so gallingly admitted, he would have done whatever was necessary to make her happy.

Meaning her happiness was much more important to him than he'd realized or, better still, understood.

He didn't know quite what to make of that and was disinclined to do the necessary internal excavation to uncover the rationale behind the observation. He grimly suspected one revelation would lead to another and he'd wind up more damned enlightened than he was prepared to deal with at the moment.

His mood blackened.

What he could deal with, however, was Jason and all the other lying bastards who'd broken their pledges to her. And to the clinic. And to all the people who depended on the clinic for their medical care. Marion was smart. She wouldn't have wasted her time asking for donations from individuals or companies she knew couldn't afford it.

People like Jason, whose newfound wealth hadn't been able to buy him any class.

Robin slid into the driver's seat, pulled out his cell phone and called John. "You still with Jason?"

"I am," John said around what was obviously a mouthful of food. "We're at Carnival Cuisine where Jason has kindly arranged for me to taste everything on the menu. I'm not even halfway through yet."

"Good. Take your time then," he told him. "I'm coming over there. I need to have a little chat with Jason." John knew him well enough to know that, from the tone of his voice, "little chat" was synonymous with an ass-kicking.

His friend's silence stretched briefly across the line. "Is that right? And why is that?"

Robin filled him in. "She's been going out with him, trying to get him to pony up the donation he'd promised. She's doing it for the clinic, John. And according to Marion, there are many, many more."

"I see," John said. "Would I be correct in assuming that you're going to have a *little chat* with everyone who has failed to make good on their promises, as well?"

"That would be a fair assumption, yes."

"Excellent. Count me in."

Robin grinned. "I already had."

"You know the Red Ball is tomorrow night, right? I imagine that a good number of the people who've ended up on Marion's list will be there. Perhaps instead of using the sledgehammer approach—not that it isn't effective, mind you—you should employ a more…considered method. You've got Ranger Security resources at your fingertips, after all. Who knows what sort of leverage might emerge from a little reconnaissance."

The Red Ball was an annual event hosted by Partners for Progress, a coalition of wealthy businessmen who believed in the old I'll-scratch-your-back-if-you-scratch-mine approach to industry. It took place at the Turtledove, one of the oldest and grandest hotels in the downtown area and was one of the premiere formal events of the year for the city's elite. It was a black-tie occasion and, true to its namesake, the women all wore red. It made a striking impression.

"The Red Ball?" Robin heard Jason say. "I'm going to the Red Ball. I'm told it's quite exclusive."

Robin snorted. Not exclusive enough if that jackass got an invitation.

"It is," John told him. "You've got your red tuxedo already, don't you? Those damned things are rare. I had to have mine special made. Double breasted with big brass buttons."

Robin guffawed, thankful that Jason couldn't hear him. "Don't forget the gold cord."

John dutifully added the cord and then told Jason that if he really wanted to make the right impression, he should consider a matching hat, as well. "Women love hats. It's the mark of a gentleman."

"You are evil, my friend," Robin said, chuckling. "Brilliant, but evil."

"Likewise. See you in a bit."

Robin disconnected and, on a whim, sent a quick text to Ranger's resident hacker, Charlene "Charlie" Weatherford. He liked everyone he worked with, but he was especially fond of Charlie and her husband, Jay. They were new parents and sickeningly in love.

Rather than text back, she called him. "I wasn't busy at all. Just bored. What do you need?"

"Bored? How can you be bored with a toddler underfoot?"

"Both the toddler and my husband have gone to bed, there's nothing worth watching on television and Juan-Carlos's emails have taken a turn toward the mundane."

Juan-Carlos was the superefficient office manager who had perfected the art of looking simultaneously martyred and put-upon. While everyone else seemed to understand that Charlie didn't understand the word *private,* the little Latino man didn't, and would flip a bitch if he knew Charlie had been hacking into his email account.

"Please tell me you need me to do something," she implored, sounding a bit like an addict jonesing for a fix.

Robin grinned. "I do, actually." He outlined what he needed. "Is that going to present a problem?"

She feigned insult. "Please," she said. "It's child's play. Are you sure that's all you need?"

"For the moment, though I'll probably need additional assistance tomorrow. Will you be around?"

"I will," she said.

"Excellent."

He disconnected, then started the car and, with one last lingering look at Marion's pink fortress, he backed out of the driveway.

It was time to deal with Jason.

He'd take care of Marion in the morning. Whatever she intended with that house, she'd made a tactical error.

He wasn't afraid of pink.

5

Justine skidded to a stop just inside Marion's door and beamed strangely at her. It was the same manic, starstruck smile her right-hand-woman only wore for one person.

Robin.

"He's here," she said, her voice stuck between breathless and squeaky. "I just saw him pull up." Her eyes rounded in surprise. "Did you know that he got a new truck? It's one of those four-door jobs with a big tow hitch and running boards. And it's *dirty,*" she said, as though this was especially of note.

Actually, she did know about the truck because that was what he'd driven her home in last night, though she hadn't noticed it being dirty or having a tow hitch. Of course, she'd been too keenly aware of him to pay much attention to anything else. She just remembered that it smelled like him—warm and fragrant, like patchouli and sandalwood. His scent had lingered long after he'd left and she'd found herself reluctant to wash her face, irrationally not wanting to rinse away his kiss. Her skin tingled anew just thinking about it, and an arc of heat blossomed deep in her belly.

From a seemingly harmless kiss on the cheek, and yet...
And yet nothing could have made her want him more.

Wasn't this why she'd avoided him? Why she'd been careful to never be alone with him? Because she couldn't trust herself. Because everything about Robin Sherwood drew her in. The mischievous, intelligent eyes, the lazy grin, that wicked sense of humor.

And then there was more—the substantial things. Character, for example. That antiquated notion that a man should honor his word—or a bet, she thought wryly, remembering his outfit from last night. One who would let his "yes" be "yes" and his "no" a "no." One who could afford a mansion, but lived in an idyllic farmhouse instead. One who was here this morning to make others keep *their* word, honor *their* promises. That's the kind of man Robin Sherwood was, the kind that, regrettably, made every other guy pale in comparison.

She was doomed, Marion thought. Doomed to care too much about a man whose grandfather was ultimately responsible for the death of her brother and the ruination of her family. Rationally, she knew that Robin wasn't to blame—he'd been just a kid himself—but she'd be lying if she said the association wasn't always going to be a stumbling block.

And even if she could get past it, she knew her mother couldn't.

Her mother had never set foot in the clinic, simply because it was funded with Sherwood money. Her logic didn't exactly make sense considering everything about her existence—including the retirement she currently enjoyed and which Marion supplemented—was funded with Sherwood money. Her mother had badgered Marion for years about quitting the clinic and doing something different, something that would permanently sever ties with the Sherwood family, but Marion had never been able to do that. She was happy here, and she did good work. Work that honored her brother...and kept her as close as she was able to be to Robin.

She wasn't sure which motivation was more powerful and feared too much introspection on the subject would reveal a truth she didn't particularly want to face.

Justine bustled over, pulled open one of Marion's desk drawers and removed a forgotten tube of lip gloss. "Hold still," she said, determinedly aiming the application wand at Marion's lips.

Startled, Marion shrugged back and scowled at her. "I can do that myself, thanks," she said. "If I thought I needed it," she added. "Which I don't." Honestly, Marion thought. This wasn't a date, for pity's sake. He was simply coming by to pick up a list. Nothing more. So why was her heart threatening to beat out of her chest, and why was her previously calm stomach staging a coup?

"Yes, you do," Justine told her. "Trust me, bloodless lips aren't attractive. You need some color."

Ordinarily Marion would have dismissed Justine's remark out of hand because Justine, a fit fifty who subscribed to the "more is more" philosophy of makeup, was forever trying to offer beauty tips. Marion loved color as much as anyone, but when it came to applying it to her face, she preferred a more natural look. She hesitated, torn. But if her lips were indeed "bloodless," then admittedly that was *not* attractive and she was just vain enough to want to remedy the problem.

"Fine," she said, taking the gloss. "But I'll do it myself."

Justine beamed at her, evidently thrilled to be making some progress. "Excellent." She pulled a compact of blush from her pocket. "While you're at it, you might as well add a little—"

"No."

The woman's face fell. "Just a little to accentuate—"

A knock at the door frame prevented further argument and possible bodily injury to her assistant. "Morning, ladies. I'm not interrupting anything, am I?" Robin asked, looking delicious as always.

He wore a sage-green pullover that brought out the matching color in his hazel eyes, a pair of worn jeans that would no doubt showcase his prize-winning ass and a pair of leather boots that put her in mind of the old phrase "size matters." What little moisture remained in her mouth fled to parts south of her navel with alarming rapidity. Good Lord…

He'd obviously shaved this morning, but had missed a teensy spot just to the left of the cleft on his chin and, for whatever reason—insanity, most likely—she found that unbelievably endearing.

"Not at all," Justine replied, a too-bright smile pasted on her lips. She shoved the blush back into her pocket with all the subtlety of a teenager hiding a forbidden pack of cigarettes, then awkwardly patted Marion on the shoulder and shot her a conspiratorial glance. "Just finishing up a chat."

Marion ought to know better than to be mortified, but a blush betrayed her all the same.

Looking a bit bemused, Robin watched her assistant sail out of the room and then found her gaze once more. "Justine's…the same," he finished, evidently unable to come up with a better description.

Marion sympathized.

"That she is," she agreed, resisting the urge to massage her temples. She looked up and smiled. "Good morning."

He sauntered forward and, looking more than a little pleased with himself, carefully laid a check on top of her desk. A quick glance confirmed it was from Jason…and it was double the amount of his original pledge. A smile flirted with her lips.

Only Robin.

"Thank you," she said, grinning up at him. Irrationally pleased—hell, it wasn't like he'd slain a damned dragon—she poked her tongue in her cheek and slid the check into her top drawer. "You made quick work of that."

He settled his six-and-a-half-foot muscled frame into the smallish chair in front of her desk and somehow managed to appear comfortable. "I talked to him before I went home last night."

"Talked?" she queried skeptically. "Did he acquire any bruises during this particular conversation?"

Robin's warm chuckle matched his good-humored gaze. "Only to his ego, I assure you. Though I was prepared to make him see reason in any number of ways, had he not been so cooperative," he added in a grimmer tone.

She'd just bet he was. And the very idea made her foolish heart thrill at the thought of each one. It was downright...bloodthirsty. What the hell was wrong with her? And if it was wrong, then why did it feel so right?

"As promised, here's the list," she said, handing him the file she'd pulled together early this morning.

He accepted it without looking at it, which she didn't question but thought was strange considering it was supposed to be the reason he was here this morning. "Thanks," he told her. "Do you have plans for this evening?"

Marion blinked and her pathetic heart jumped into her throat. Her? Plans? Only if watching reruns of *The Big Bang Theory* and painting her toenails passed for plans. "Er, I—"

He gestured to the folder. "I'm guessing that the bulk of the people on this list will be at the Red Ball tonight, and I was hoping you'd accompany me." He grinned at her. "We can tag team them, make them pay up."

Ah, Marion thought, her own smile frozen. Actually,

she preferred her own plans for the evening, such as they were, to attending a formal event with people who paid more for their lawn care than her annual salary. But technically, it was part of her job. And since Robin had already proved he could make reluctant pledges honor their promises, how could she refuse? It was for the good of the clinic, right? And watching him in action would no doubt be entertaining and gratifying.

Frankly, only the possibility of doing more harm than good for the clinic had kept her from taking a more forceful approach to collecting the outstanding pledges. Robin was better connected, better insulated and could do much more in that regard than she could.

She nodded. "Sounds good. I'll meet you there." This was a slippery slope and she was clinging determinedly to the edge. She didn't trust herself enough to allow him another home visit. Intuition told her if Robin crossed her threshold again, he'd be doing more than breaching her inner sanctum, he'd be invading—with her full cooperation—her bedroom, as well.

From the moment she'd seen him last night, every bit of forgotten longing and unresolved sexual frustration had boiled to the surface, making her feel feverish and jittery, spun up and wound tight. Like a coiled spring ready to snap. Every moment spent in his company only compounded the issue and eroded what little remained of her self-control.

Robin stilled for a fraction of a second, his easy smile turning brittle. "I've just invited you to the Red Ball and you said yes. It's a date, Marion," he explained with exaggerated patience. "I'll pick you up."

The breath in her lungs thinned. A date? Well, yes, by that definition she supposed it was. Her head spun. A date. Right. She cleared her throat, tried to gather her fractured thoughts. "Part of the service, is it?" she asked, her voice weak.

He smiled, the corner of his mouth hitching into that grin she couldn't resist. "In a manner of speaking."

A date…

God help her. She was *so* going to need some divine intervention.

WELL, THAT CERTAINLY HADN'T gone as planned, Robin thought as Marion led him through the clinic. Though he could tell she'd made various improvements and, as usual, had everything as efficient and streamlined as possible, he could barely hear her from the noise in his own head.

Date? Yes, he'd asked her to go with him to the Red Ball, more as a ploy to get to spend some more time with her—and to show off, if he was honest, because he'd devised some pretty devious ways to get people to part with their promised money—he hadn't actually meant it to be a genuine honest-to-goodness *date.*

At least, he didn't think he did, but at this point, who the hell knew? Perspective—if he'd ever had any to begin with—had gone by the wayside. He just knew that when she'd offered to meet him—*meet him,* for crying out loud—at the venue…something had just snapped inside him. Her determination to keep him at arm's length, even when he was trying to help her, galled him to no end.

She might as well have waved a red flag in front of a bull.

While "retreat" might be in other men's character, it wasn't in his.

Her little attempt to dodge him only made him want to advance and reload. Made him want to grab hold of the long braid presently bobbing between her shoulder blades and tug her to him, then lick the sweet spot on the back of her neck. She was in another long and flowing dress today, this one a dark purple with a fitted bodice that fully covered her breasts, but somehow managed to display them to perfect advantage anyway. The color accentuated her pale skin, made it glow, even in this horrendous commercial light.

And the way she moved… She didn't just walk. She *glided,* head high and swanlike.

It was sexy as hell.

"Marion," Justine called down the hallway they were currently exploring. She winced regrettably. "I hate to interrupt, but Gage is here again and insists on seeing you."

Marion's smile dimmed. She stilled and some unspoken communication passed between the two women. She nodded. "Show him into my office, would you, Justine?" She turned to Robin. "I'm afraid this is going to conclude our tour, unless you'd like to wait."

Oh, he'd wait, if for no other reason than to find out who this Gage was and why he thought he could insist on anything when it came to Marion. "I'll just grab a cup of coffee in the lounge."

She nodded, seemingly pleased. "I'll only be a few minutes."

Robin had just reached the lounge door when Justine and a scrawny teenaged boy came into view. The kid's clothes were worn, but clean, and his shaggy ginger hair looked as if a blind barber had gotten a hold of it. He put Robin in mind of a poor man's Christopher Robin. Marion smiled warmly when she saw him, then ran a hand down the boy's woefully thin back. Before Robin could read anymore into the exchange, they disappeared into her office. Justine's usually perky face was wreathed in a sad frown, which she instantly transformed when she caught Robin watching.

She bustled forward. "Let me get you that cup of coffee while you're waiting," she said. "It should only be a few minutes."

"It looked more serious than a few minutes," he remarked. "Is that boy sick? Does he have an illness?"

Justine topped off a cup and handed it to him. "No, he's as well as he can be, all things considered."

Well, that was cryptic enough. Intrigued, Robin leaned a hip against the counter. "Oh? What things?"

"His mother is a former prostitute with end-stage AIDS and a bad drug habit. She's never been a patient here, but from what I've heard, she trades whatever assistance she gets to feed her habit and not her son. Gage has been removed from the home several times by Children's Services, but he invariably runs away and goes back to her. He says he has to take care of her, that she doesn't have anyone else." Justine swallowed. "That's true, of course. But it's a damned shame that he's got a better sense of responsibility than his own mother does." She looked up and her gaze met Robin's. "Because that boy doesn't have anyone, either…other than Marion."

Robin didn't have any idea what he'd expected Justine to say, but this certainly wasn't it. He swallowed, sickened. What a burden to put on a kid's shoulders. "How old is he?"

"Thirteen."

"And he hasn't contracted the disease?"

"No. He's tested every three months and Marion has gone over all the safety issues with him. He's smart. He understands."

"So why is he here?"

"Work, most likely. He does odd jobs around the clinic. Marion pays him to sweep, take out the garbage, that sort of thing." She grinned. "Last week she had him planting flowers. He tried to pretend like he was mortified, but I think he secretly enjoyed it."

"What about school?"

"He goes when he can and his teachers work with him. Children's Services is turning a blind eye for the time being." She hesitated. "Shannon's days are limited."

"And what's going to happen to him then?"

Justine released a long breath and shook her head. "I have no idea. And for the record, when I say she pays him, I mean *she* pays him. Out of her own pocket, not out of the clinic's account. A good portion of her salary is reserved for what she calls her 'discretionary fund.'"

Well, that certainly explained a lot, Robin thought, not the least bit surprised. That was Marion. Generous, caring, invested. Siphoning off part of her own earnings to help people less fortunate than she was, but doing it in a way that taught a good work ethic and wasn't demeaning.

Amazing.

Justine glanced up at Robin. "And there are many others just like him. Different stories, but with the same circumstances. She's an angel of mercy, that girl. We're lucky to have her."

Yes, Robin thought. *Yes, they were.*

"You wouldn't happen to have a list of the people she helps, would you?"

Justine's heavily made-up gaze turned shrewd, then she grinned. "No, but I'd be happy to make one for you. Confidentially, of course."

"Of course." He made a quick decision. "Rather than tie up anymore of Marion's time, I'm going to go on. Tell her goodbye for me, please, and that I'll see her at six-thirty." He grinned. "Oh, and tell her to wear red."

6

WHATEVER RESERVATIONS MARION might have had about her Red Ball attire were completely alleviated when she opened her door and Robin's jaw literally dropped.

She laughed, delighted. "Just let me get my purse," she said, "and I'm ready to go."

Robin followed her in. "Go? Are we meant to go somewhere?" He gave his head a small shake. "I've completely forgotten."

"What's on the menu for this event?" Marion asked him, beyond flattered. "I didn't have time to eat and I'm starving."

His gaze slid from one end of her body to the other and he licked his lips. Impossibly, she felt the slide of his tongue...*everywhere.* "Me, too."

Her belly flipped over and a current of heat slid into her loins. Her breasts pouted behind her bra. Marion released a shaky breath. "And that's the first of what I imagine will be many Big Bad Wolf impressions for the evening."

"It's the cape," he said, eyes twinkling. "Although I seriously doubt Little Red Riding Hood was as lovely as you are."

She blushed at the compliment, more so than usual because she knew it was sincere. She could tell by the way he looked at her, like she was the appetizer, main course and dessert all rolled into one. It was thrilling. "Thank you. You don't look half-bad yourself," she said, gesturing to his evening wear. He wore a simple black tux which had obviously been handmade to size, it fit him so well. He was clean shaven, his tawny curls smoothed into place.

"Only half-bad?" he lamented with a feigned wince. "I was hoping for full bad. Full bad is so much better, after all."

She chewed the inside of her cheek. "You look quite handsome," she told him. "What? No hat tonight?" she quipped.

"I only bring that out for special occasions."

She grinned, nodded, then lifted the edge of her velvet cape and let the fabric slip through her fingers. "That's how I feel about my cape. You said to wear red."

"I did," he concurred with an appreciative nod. "And you wear it so well."

It was nothing but pure dumb luck that she had it at all, but she'd stumbled upon the designer dress and matching cape while clicking her way through an online auction site. It was her size, her price and she'd been waiting for an occasion to wear it. Admittedly, it made her feel sexy. The dress itself was a simple satin sheath with a sweetheart neckline and a modest slit up the side. The cape, however, also satin-lined, was what made the outfit so dramatic. Yards and yards of red silk and velvet with a generous, cord-rimmed hood.

It was gorgeous and, more importantly, it made her feel gorgeous.

As a hat tip to Justine, she'd even applied matching lipstick and nail polish.

Angus sauntered into the living room and tried to curl

around her legs. "Oh, no, you," she said, guiltily sidestepping out of his reach. "I spent thirty minutes with the lint brush and don't have time for another run at it."

Angus blinked up at her, looking wounded enough to make Robin chuckle.

"Does that look often work?"

"Regrettably, yes."

"Then I'll need to take lessons." He arched a brow. "What sort of cat is he? I don't think I've ever seen one like him before."

Marion smiled and looked indulgently down at her pet. "At least you recognize that he's a breed. Most people think he's got some sort of birth defect." She glanced up. "He's a Scottish Fold. I got him when I moved in. Mom would never let us have a pet. She said animals were meant to be outdoors."

Robin grimaced. "My grandfather would never let us have anything, either. He didn't want to deal with food costs and vet bills. But I'm slowly populating the farm. I've got a few cows, a couple of horses, chickens, ducks and geese. And I've got a black-and-white border collie named Oreo—previous owner's doing, not mine—that's a bed hog."

Her lips twisted. "Oreo, huh?"

He opened the door for her and they descended the steps. "John calls her Cookie just to piss me off."

"John does a lot of things just to piss you off. Will he be there tonight?" she asked as she slid into the passenger seat.

"He will. He's helping us." And with that cryptic comment, he closed her door and rounded the hood. "Trust me," he said as he slid behind the wheel. "You're going to be mightily entertained this evening."

"That's not particularly comforting," Marion murmured, equally anticipating and dreading what was to come. She had a sneaking suspicion that her entertainment was going to double as someone else's embarrassment.

And that misgiving was confirmed the instant they walked into the ballroom. "Oh, dear Lord," Marion breathed, stifling the urge to howl with laughter. "What did you do to Jason?"

Robin grinned, devilment dancing in his gaze, and blinked innocently. "Whatever do you mean?"

Jason was the only man in the room dressed in a red… suit? Tuxedo? Something. It was tricked out with lots of big brass buttons and yards of golden chord and tassels, but the hat… She covered her mouth as a giggle escaped her. The hat was the kicker. It was round, with a small bill edged in more ghastly golden chord. It made him look like a bellhop, which was no doubt why people kept handing him their drinks. Presently, he had two champagne flutes in one hand, two in the other, and another tucked up under his arm.

His face matched the outfit, either from embarrassment or anger. Or hell, probably both.

"Excuse me," Marion said, darting behind a potted palm so that she could laugh properly. Her sides and shoulders shook and her eyes watered, which ordinarily wouldn't have mattered, but she'd applied mascara and didn't want to make a mess of her face.

She felt Robin come up behind her, his big hand on her shoulder. "You okay?" he asked, his own voice shaking with repressed merriment.

"Fine," she breathed through another chuckle, and turned to scold him. "I can't believe you did that. That poor man. He'll be the butt of jokes for y-years to c-come."

"Yes, he will, which is appropriate in my opinion because he's an *ass.* And he deserves it." He nodded sagely. "A little humility would do Jason a whole lot of good."

She glanced up at him, her eyes wide with sarcasm. "Oh, and you're the person who should deliver that message? You, the same man who thought you could put an arrow through a moving tire swing while drunk?" Her eyebrows rose. "*You're* the one who should be teaching him humility?"

"Hey, I took my punishment, didn't I?" he asked, feigning outrage. He gestured toward the red-faced Jason, who was juggling even more glasses. "This is merely his." He nudged her shoulder and grinned. "Admit it. It's funny."

She stifled another wicked giggle and shook her head. "It is funny."

"And this is only the beginning. Thirteen of the twenty-two that are on the list will be here tonight and I've got a little something planned for each and every one of them."

Ah. "Is that what the duffel bag you hid under our table is for?"

His lips twitched. "You weren't meant to see that."

"But I did."

"Oh, look, there's John!" he said as if he'd never seen him before in his life, then grabbed her elbow and propelled her forward.

A thought struck. "Twenty-two?" she said, frowning. "The list I gave you only had nineteen people on it."

"We'll talk about that later."

"Talk about what later?" Marion asked, her brow furrowing in confusion. "Where did the other names come from if I didn't give them to you?"

Robin nodded and smiled his way across the ballroom, making a beeline for John. "From your files."

"My files? The clinic's files?" She blinked. "But how did you—"

"I used a source at Ranger Security to help me out last night. I didn't want to wait to start my research."

Her head was spinning. Ranger Security? Start his research? Realization dawned and she gasped and dug in her heels. So that was why he didn't seem concerned with the list this morning—because he already had it. "You hacked me?" she hissed. "You hacked into my system?"

Swallowing what appeared to be several oaths, he took a deep breath and looked down at her. "The clinic's system, yes. And not me, precisely, but another agent from the firm. We're going to need to update your security," he added as an aside. "According to Charlie, you're firewall is a joke."

She wasn't sure what was more alarming—that he'd hacked her or that he'd been able to. "Really, Robin, that wasn't—"

He leveled a look at her. "Is there anything at all in there that I wouldn't be allowed to see?"

That took a bit of the self-righteous wind out of her sails. She wavered. "Of course not. I just don't appreciate your methods."

To her surprise, he dropped a quick kiss on the tip of her nose and grinned at her. "Not yet, maybe," he said. "But I bet you will."

Her nose still tingling, her stomach in knots, she tsked shakily under her breath. "You and those bets. Who's the slow learner now?"

He took her hand once more—warm, callused palm, strong fingers—and resumed their trek across the ballroom. "I'm not a slow learner," he said. "I'm merely stubborn."

"There's a difference?"

"It's subtle."

She snorted softly. "There are many things about you,

Robin Sherwood, but subtle is definitely *not* a word I'd use to describe your character."

He stopped suddenly and looked down at her, a question in his heavily lashed hazel eyes. His lashes were gold-tipped, Marion realized now, her breath caught in her throat. Like they'd been dipped in paint. Funny how she'd never noticed that before.

"Oh? Then how would you describe me, Marion?" he asked, his voice low and slightly roughened, an odd undercurrent just below the surface.

She faltered beneath that concentrated intensity, as though her answer really mattered, carried more weight than it should. She blinked, suddenly terrified. Of what, she couldn't begin to fathom. She only knew this moment was too…much. And that her future happiness might possibly hinge on her answer.

How would she describe him? Wonderful, honorable, trustworthy, wicked, mischievous, hot, honest, loyal, decent, gorgeous, fun, clever, brilliant, brave, generous, unique…perfect. But she didn't have the courage to say any of those things.

"At the moment…heavy," she said, wincing in pain.

His gaze clouded in perplexity. "What? Heavy?"

"Yes, heavy," she repeated, giving him a little push. "You're on my foot."

His eyes widened, then he jumped back and grinned sheepishly, the moment gone. Charming, irreverent Robin had returned as though the other guy, the one who'd been oddly…vulnerable just a moment ago had never existed. "Sorry," he said. "Do you want me to kiss it and make it better?"

"I bet he won't do it," John announced in carrying tones. When the hell had he arrived on the scene? "A thousand dollars." He glanced around, his face split in a big grin. "Any takers?"

She could cheerfully throttle him, Marion thought. Bets between the two friends was one thing—making her a party to it was another. And it was her damned foot! Would she like for Robin to kiss her feet? Yes, yes, a thousand times yes. A bit of groveling wouldn't be remiss, either, if she was perfectly honest. But given her choice, that particular area wouldn't be the first place she'd want him to start, that was for damned sure.

Marion felt her smile freeze. "That won't be necessary, John. You can keep your money. I'm fine."

John's eyes twinkled with unrepentant humor. "You don't have to be tough, Marion. The oaf just planted his two-hundred-and-ten-pound, size-twelve foot on your dainty little toes. A kiss would surely make them feel better."

Truth be told, she was more in danger of hurting her foot by planting it up John's ass. She glared at him, her voice hard. "I'm fine, really."

"Two thousand," John said, his gaze and smile equally steady.

Robin turned to Marion and arched a playful brow. She recognized that look and knew exactly what it meant. "I'll split the money with you," he offered.

John had little to no regard for her foot or whether or not she was genuinely hurt—he merely wanted to make mischief. And, much like Justine, she imagined, *matchmake.*

Marion swung a speculative gaze at John, taking his measure, then lifted her chin and deliberately extended her foot. "Get your wallet out, big man. I could use an extra grand."

To Marion's surprise, a whoop of *ooo-la-la* laughter met her bold statement. Naturally, much to her chagrin, they'd attracted quite an audience. But when did Robin and John not attract attention? Not make a scene or create some sort of spectacle? Wasn't that what she secretly loved about them? That they were fun and outrageous? That they didn't take themselves too seriously? That they were somehow bigger and burned more brightly than everyone else around them?

What would it hurt, really, to bask in their reflected glow?

Robin shot John a smug look, then turned that twinkling gaze on her. Admiration clung to his wicked smile, making her irrational heart skip a beat and, with all of the ceremony of Prince Charming attending to Cinderella's glass slipper, he flipped his coat tail back and sank to one knee. She was keenly aware of his mouth in proximity to another part of her anatomy and that part clenched and slickened as awareness blossomed through her. Her pulse hammered through her veins, her mouth parched.

Too late she realized her mistake, the flaw in her thinking.

Even in Robin's reflected glow, she could get burned.

He reached for the back of her leg, just her calf and the feel of his warm, strong hand against her skin—any skin, evidently—made her entire body tingle with pinpricks of pleasant sensation. She inhaled inaudibly, determined to keep the unconcerned I-just-want-my-grand smile on her face, but internally every cell was energized and hypersensitive.

Internally, she was crumbling.

Though he appeared every bit as cool and calm as she did, gratifyingly Marion perceived the slightest tremor in his fingers, a tiny but significant betrayal of his own desire. A crack in the armor, thank God, because she didn't want to be the only one falling apart. She wanted him to crumble as well, to burn as she did. He slid his hand almost reverently along the back of her leg, lifting it up so that he could remove her shoe and the sensation was unbelievably erotic, bone-shatteringly carnal.

He glanced up at her, his gaze hot and desperate, an unspoken invitation to sin, then bent his tawny head and placed a lingering kiss on the top of her foot. She dimly noted the catcalls and applause, the raucous laughter and whoops of admiration. The rest of the room faded away, shrunk into nothingness, and all that was left was the man kneeling before her, his talented lips against her naked flesh. And not even on one of the better parts, like her mouth or her neck or her breasts or her belly. Just his lips on her foot. She was relatively certain that a slip of his tongue along her ankle would facilitate an immaculate orgasm.

Right here. At the Red Ball. In front of witnesses.

Marion released a shaky breath as he carefully slipped her shoe back on, then released another when he lowered her foot back to the floor. So she wasn't floating then? Right. Good to know.

And she'd been worried about letting him drive her home? Clearly Robin Sherwood was dangerous no matter where they were. And it wasn't fear pushing her heart rate into overdrive—it was excitement.

7

Over the years Robin had done his share of disrobing a partner. He'd learned how to covertly snap open a bra at fourteen, how to soundlessly lower a zipper at fifteen. He'd mastered the art of removing pesky clothing inch by inch until nothing remained but a pair of panties and, typically, by the time they'd reached that stage in the seduction, she was taking those off herself.

In a nutshell, he was experienced.

But no amount of experience could have prepared him for the utter meltdown of sensation he'd undergone from simply lifting Marion's leg, removing her shoe and placing a kiss on the top of her foot. It didn't matter that they were surrounded by a room full of people—most notably, John, with his keen eyes. When he'd touched her—when his palm had rested against her creamy bare skin—his entire body, from the inside out, had felt it. He'd *shook* from the power of it, had practically rattled the damned fillings in his teeth.

And he'd only touched her leg, only kissed her cheek and her nose and her elegant foot. When he finally kissed her on the mouth—which he fully intended to do tonight—

he'd undoubtedly self-combust. But he was too far gone now to care.

Because this was Marion—*his* Marion—and God help him, he wanted her.

His gaze tangled with hers, those ice-blue eyes dilated with desire, her mouth open in silent invitation, and it took every bit of restraint he possessed to merely smile at her and carry on. He darted a look at John. "Cash, my friend. No checks."

Looking entirely too pleased with himself, John merely chuckled. "You know I'm good for it."

"And I know where you live."

John arched a meaningful brow and gestured to a person across the room. "What do you say? Shall we get started?"

Robin followed his gaze and felt his own narrow. Ah, yes. Lester Holland, the number-one offender on Marion's list. Pledged one hundred thousand dollars in support of the clinic a year and a half ago and had yet to relinquish one red cent. A quick peek into Lester's financial data revealed that his business was booming. Lester's company manufactured many things, but most significantly roofing shingles.

After the particularly harsh tornado season, most notably in Alabama, Lester's product had been in high demand. So high, in fact, that Lester's company had been accused of price gouging. The accusation had gone away—money had a way of solving those kind of problems—but given the evidence Robin had seen, Lester would have had a hard time proving his innocence. Robin smiled grimly.

The man was about to part with some of his ill-gotten gains.

Marion touched his arm and leaned in. "Why are you glaring at Lester Holland?" she asked suspiciously.

He turned to look at her and arched a meaningful brow. "You'll see. I'll be back in a few minutes."

Leaving an anxious Marion, Robin wound his way through the ballroom, while a covert look at John revealed he'd gotten into position with their prop. Robin had been aware that Ranger Security's research capabilities were top-notch, but he hadn't realized just how good they were until he'd started his own project. With Charlie's help, Robin had been able to uncover a particularly *peculiar* fetish that Lester and several more on the list here tonight shared.

They liked to drink breast milk. Directly from the breast, preferably while wearing a diaper.

Lester had his very own adult-sized nursery—Robin wouldn't have believed it if he hadn't seen the video feed Charlie had found—complete with a playpen and baby bed. And he kept a rotation of lactating donors, for lack of a better description, who came around once a week and…fed the men.

Some of America's wealthiest, most successful men… and they liked to wear diapers, nurse and get spanked.

It boggled the mind.

But it made for damned good blackmail.

Though it took a few minutes of idle chitchat, he was able to maneuver the group into a private circle, then with a few veiled comments, which left them all slack-jawed and terrified, he directed their attention to John, who beamingly held up a bottle of milk and a pacifier. "Listen, gentlemen, to each his own I say," Robin told them in his best good-old-Georgia-boy voice. "People like what they like and there's no accounting for taste. But do you know what leaves a bad taste in my mouth?" His voice hardened and he leveled a lethal stare at each one of them. "Liars," he said. "People who break promises. Specifically, to one charity organization which is close to my heart." His gaze moved significantly to Marion and he waited until each one of them looked at her and made the connection. "Double your pledge amounts and courier payment over by 9:00 a.m. tomorrow morning. The price of my silence triples for every minute that it's late." He slapped Lester on the back and grinned at him, though the humor didn't reach his eyes. "Am I making myself clear?"

Robin didn't wait for their answer, merely moved on to the next target, a local professional baseball player who enjoyed the drag queen scene in the off-season. Not here, of course—there was too much potential for recognition—but he was familiar with all the lovely ladies in New Orleans. His stage name was Roxanne Rococco, but everyone called him Rocki for short. John glanced significantly at Rocki, then pretended to apply a bit of lipstick.

Rocki paled and assured his cooperation.

Next was the city councilman who was having an affair with his secretary, which wouldn't have been remarkable if said council member wasn't married to a high-profile female pastor and said council member's secretary had been a woman.

Robin had just convinced the last person on his list—for tonight anyway—to cooperate when the band struck up Chris De Burgh's "The Lady In Red." His gaze instantly sought out his own lady in red and a bizarre sensation winged through his suddenly tight chest as his gaze connected with hers.

Twinkling ice-blue eyes, the carnal curve of shockingly red mouth, the elegant slope of her cheek. Creamy skin, jet-black hair spilling over her pale shoulders. All wrapped up in a sexy package of red satin and velvet.

She was beautiful. Heart-stoppingly, breathtakingly stunning.

And so damned hot, he ached for her, burned for her.

His feet seemed to move of their own volition, casually eating up the distance between the two of them. Smiling, he drew her to him, her hand in his, tucked against his chest, the other firmly around her slim waist. She smelled delicious—warm and flowery, like a hot summer night from so long ago—and he breathed her in. He went instantly hard, which she couldn't help but notice.

She stilled for a fraction of a second and he felt the muscles tighten in her lower back. A beat slid to three before she relaxed. She wrapped a hand around his neck, her fingers playing with the hair of his nape and a little mewling sound of contentment slipped past her lips.

Another wall brought down, Robin thought, breathing a silent sigh of relief.

"You seem quite pleased with yourself," she remarked as they swayed to the music.

"You'll be pleased with me tomorrow morning," he said, purposely, whispering in her ear.

She shivered and her eyes fluttered shut. "Oh?"

He held her closer. "Just wait. It's a surprise."

"Is it a surprise that's going to get me secretly blacklisted with every potential contributor in the greater Atlanta area?"

"Please," he said. "Give me a little credit, would you? I'd never put your reputation—or that of the clinic's—in jeopardy. If anyone is stupid enough to so much as scowl at you, they'll answer to me. And they'll regret it," he added darkly.

She was quiet for a few seconds, so long that he wished that he had some sort of telepathic ability so that he could read her mind, to know what was going on in that fascinating little head of hers. "I really don't think I have to worry about it," she said, a smile in her voice. "Lester

Holland looked terrified when I spoke to him earlier, and Martin Jones literally turned and walked in the other direction when he saw me coming his way." She shook her head, evidently baffled. "I was only going to the refreshment table. I wasn't even looking for him. Fool," she muttered, mildly outraged.

A smile tugged at his lips. "They're only allowed to communicate with you through their checkbooks," Robin told her, finding her indignation adorable. "Which is what's important, right?"

She nodded against him, her hair tickling his chin. "Right. So I worked out the significance of most everything in the duffel bag, but I have to admit that the baby bottle and pacifier threw me. Can you elaborate?"

He hesitated. "Er…are you sure you want me to?" he asked, a skeptical warning in his voice.

She drew back and looked up at him, intrigue lighting her crystalline gaze. "Well, now I *have* to know, though I'm guessing I'll probably regret it."

"You will," he assured her. "But if you really want to know." He filled her in, watched as her expression went from purely icked out to utterly revolted. He sympathized.

"Wow," she said, evidently trying to blink away the mental picture. "Just…wow."

"I warned you," he said.

She continued to blink, her countenance oddly blank. "You did."

The song ended and he reluctantly released her, but held on to her hand. It was small and graceful, but capable and strong and it felt inexplicably…right in his. He gestured toward the veranda. "Why don't we get some air?"

Air was wonderful, but admittedly he had an ulterior motive. One that involved him and her and the moonlight. He couldn't wait to see what she'd look like in it. Alabaster skin, ruby lips, dark hair and that sinful red dress. A flawless combination of sexy and elegant. A Waterhouse pinup, he thought again, the description odd but fitting.

At her nod, he led her through a set of French doors. Huge potted urns, decorative fountains and statuary adorned the outdoor space, which was dotted with linen-draped tables and candlelight. Vintage gas lanterns flickered from old posts, casting wavering shadows on the smooth cement floor. Evergreen vegetation gave the appearance of an old country garden, though they were in the heart of downtown Atlanta.

"This is lovely," Marion murmured, her voice low. "I love those old gas lamps."

Robin uttered a noncommittal sound, then squeezed her hand and quickly drew around to face him. "Forgive me, Marion."

She blinked, confused, but before she could frame another word, he tipped up her chin, then framed her face with his hands and settled his mouth firmly against hers.

He staggered from the impact. The balls of his feet tingled and the sensation swept from one end of his body to the other, then made the return trek, leaving a trail of goose bumps down the back of his wobbly legs. His hands vibrated strangely, a buzzing radiating out from the center of his palms into his fingertips. His breath momentarily refused to move in and out of his paralyzed lungs and every nerve ending in his body sang from the contact.

Holy hell...

A brisk wind picked up, ruffling his hair, swirling dried leaves around the patio floor at their feet in a mini tornado, as though Mother Nature herself was affected by their energy, the sheer power of their connection.

A startled little moan issued from Marion's throat—the sweet sound of surrender—then she grabbed hold of his lapels and clung to him. Her mouth was hot and lush, her tongue tangling around his as though she'd been waiting for this as well, as though she'd been as desperate to taste him as he'd been to taste her. He wanted to lick her from one end to the other, feast on her with his mouth and his hands.

If kissing her foot had been a medal-worthy act of restraint, then dancing with her without kissing her—or hell, backing her up against the friggin' wall, for that matter—had required Herculean strength.

And he wasn't that sort of mythical hero.

Robin fed at her mouth, savored the plump fullness of her bottom lip, the feel of her gloriously rounded breasts against his chest. He shaped her ripe body more closely to his, followed the line of her spine, her hair a pleasant weight on the back of his hand. The permanent hard-on he'd been privy to for the past hour threatened to leap right out of the top of his pants, and with every savory stroke of her tongue against his, he burned even hotter. Lost just a little bit more control.

As if he'd ever had it to begin with, he thought helplessly. As if he'd ever had any control where Marion was concerned. Laughable. Insane. This was Marion, after all.

His Marion. *His* lady in red.

The only woman who'd ever gotten under his skin, wormed her way into his locked-down heart. A niggle of alarm surfaced at the thought, but he quickly squelched the sensation, determined to enjoy the moment—enjoy her—at last.

Breathing heavily, he broke away from her intoxicating mouth and trailed kisses along her jaw, along the sweet shell of her ear, and then down the swanlike column of her graceful throat, then followed the neckline of her dress along the tops of her decadent breasts with his tongue, a daring letter M.

She inhaled sharply, a gasp of pleasure, and held on to his shoulders, her fingers digging desperately into the muscles there. Need hammered through him, pummeling away at the last fleeting vestiges of his restraint. He backed her up a few steps, drew her deeper into a shadowed corner. A place for darker, sinful deeds. She clung to him, held fast, and with every pass of his lips over hers, every invasion of his tongue into her greedy mouth, he wanted her more.

Needed her more.

His dick rode high on her belly and she squirmed against him, a silent plea for release. She pushed her hands past his shoulders, around his neck, then framed his face, holding his jaw while she tasted him, her fingers reverently stroking, mesmerizing his senses. There was something intangible in her touch—something potent but unrecognizable—that just did it for him. Always had.

It drove him mad, eroded reason, robbed him of good sense.

And he wanted to take her—right here, right now. He wanted to back her up against the wall, lower her onto his aching dick and exhaust himself in her heat. He wanted to feel the rosy bud of her breast pucker in his mouth while he pushed into her, wanted to feel her hot feminine walls tighten around him, cling to him.

"Do it," Marion breathed brokenly, her voice low and smoky.

He rocked against her, desperately looking for any sort of relief, any sort of reprieve, wishing to God he'd waited until they'd at least made it to the car before kissing her. He'd planned on waiting until he drove her home—it was the gentlemanly thing to do, after all—but obviously that had been an ill-conceived idea.

"Do it," she repeated, her icy heavy-lidded gaze finding his, her lips swollen from his kiss. "Whatever you're thinking." She tore at the buttons on his shirt, baring his neck. "Do it now, Robin, and to hell with the consequences."

Clearly she had better insight into his head than he did hers, because she knew damned well what he was thinking, what he wanted. But the time to puzzle over that inequitable situation wasn't now.

She licked a trail up the side of his neck and hissed a sigh into his ear, one of the single most carnal sounds he'd ever heard. It slithered into his blood, that sibilant breath, and snapped the final thread of his admittedly thinning control.

With a guttural growl, he lifted her up, hiking her dress up in the process, and she wrapped her legs around his waist, then found his mouth once more. "I'm clean," he rasped. "Tell me you're protected."

She had to be. He couldn't wait, he had to have her.

"Clean and protected. We're good, Robin, just please—" Her kiss was desperate and demanding, mindless and insistent. A whine of a zipper and a quick nudge of her panties later, he slipped between her hot, weeping folds and thrust into her tight, welcoming heat.

Holy mother of...

He locked his knees to keep himself upright. Sensation rocketed through him, sending flames of heat licking through his veins. He shuddered, held her tighter, trying to absorb every iota of feeling, take it all in and savor each mind-blowing part of it. She sucked in a harsh breath, the sound echoing against the night, and instinctively tightened around him, claiming him, admitting defeat, owning her own need.

Robin drew back and thrust again, a masculine groan of satisfaction as he pumped into her, silently punishing her for ever trying to avoid him, for keeping him at arm's length, for refusing to let him close. He pounded harder, his hands anchored on her ripe ass. He chastised her with each frantic plunge into her soft body for painting her house pink, for not wanting to let him walk her to her door, for not wanting to let him into her home, for not wanting to let him pick her up tonight.

What had he ever done to deserve that? Robin wondered as she tightened around him, bent forward and nipped at his shoulder. He hadn't realized how much her stonewalling had bothered him until right now, until he was dick deep inside of her and *everything* seemed to matter.

Most especially, *her.*

The feel of her, the scent of her, the taste of her. She was everywhere, invading his senses, his very cells, changing his chemical makeup. He lowered his head and suckled her breast through the satin fabric of her dress, teasing the taut nipple with his tongue, and she fisted around him, triggering the first flash of his own release. He shifted, seated her more firmly against him and pumped harder, determined to make her come while chasing his own reward.

She worked herself against him, sucked at his neck, her breath coming in little mewling puffs, her hands tunneling through his hair. He squeezed her ripe ass and a strangled cry broke from her throat, every muscle in her body froze except for the ones convulsing around him, squeezing violently.

He came hard.

A guttural growl dredged from the primordial depths of his soul emerged from his mouth as he poured himself into her, each bone-racking pulse more devastating than the last. It was almost more than he could take—almost too good, if that were possible—the feeling shattering through him. It simultaneously energized and weakened him, made him want to beat his chest and roar, robbed his breath then restored it, as though she was the key to his very existence, the key to…everything.

And she was, Robin thought in a blinding moment of insight as the last twinges of release melted though him.

She was.

His breath ragged, his gaze sought and found hers. Satisfaction and awe glinted in the pale blue depths along with something else, that perpetually hidden *other* he could never quite discern.

She smiled then, her wicked mouth curving just so, and his chest squeezed with some unnamed emotion. Sated and momentarily satisfied, he bent forward and kissed her. He smiled against her lips. "The next time we do this, I promise it will be in a proper bed." A novel change, for sure, though there was something to be said for the night air and the moonlight.

She chuckled low, the sound intimate. "Excellent. How about mine?"

The invitation was issued lightly, but he recognized the significance. His gaze searched hers, pleasure swelling through him. "Yours it is, then."

For now, Robin thought. But he was going to want her in his, as well.

8

WELL, SHE'D DONE IT, MARION thought, hours later as she lay curled up against Robin's bare chest. Half a dozen frilly pillows lay forgotten on the floor of her bedroom, the red cape—which he'd insisted she put back on later—spread over them. Contentment and anxiety jockeyed for top-billing, but she ignored them both and focused instead on the warm wall of man beside her.

Tawny curls covered his chest and arrowed down his muscled abdomen, his skin a natural gold. His scent curled into her nostrils, that exotic patchouli and sandalwood fragrance that complimented his own natural aroma. She breathed him in, absently swirling doodles around his belly.

There were many valid reasons why being with him—letting him in—was not a good idea. The money issue, Michael's death, his grandfather's part in the loss of her brother, and her own mother's objections, for a start.

But lying here with him now, listening to the steady, reassuring beat of his heart beneath her ear, it was easy to forget that their relationship, if that's what this was, would be fraught with complications. She didn't want to think about those things. She just wanted to be with him. And why not? Why shouldn't she let him care for her?

Because he did. She knew it.

He cared for her in the same mindless, unwilling, terrifying, inexplicable, uncontrollable way she cared for him. He was as drawn to her as she was to him. She could read it in his eyes, which were, upon closer inspection, not quite as happy and irreverent as he'd like the world to believe.

And the most heartbreaking part? The thing that really made her ache for him? Robin didn't recognize affection, genuine love born out of warmth and regard. There'd been one blinding instant in their mad coupling against the hotel wall when she'd kissed him, stroked his face, her feelings pouring out of her fingertips, and the flash of uncertainty—the lost, quizzical look in his troubled eyes—would have driven her to her knees if he hadn't been holding her.

But why would he know anything about that sort of sentiment? Other than his father, there'd been precious little love available to him. Odd, how she used to think that money fixed everything—that if she just had enough, everything else in her world would be perfect. She pressed a kiss against his chest.

Clearly that wasn't the case and he was living, breathing proof of that. Actually, the closest thing Robin had ever had to a mother was her own, and she'd forsaken him after Michael's death.

Marion's heart constricted as an unpleasant insight surfaced—*she'd* done it, too. Other than that one night a decade ago when she'd let her feelings override her misplaced bitterness, she'd done it, too.

And she had been doing it, even now.

Self-preservation? Most certainly. Fear? Yes, a good portion of that, too. But of what? Him? When he'd never done anything but try to be close to her, to be good to her. He'd been paying for his grandfather's greediness for far too long, Marion realized. And if he'd proved anything to her over the years—and more recently—Robin Sherwood was a lot of things, but selfish wasn't one of them.

He'd made it his mission to right her wrongs, to collect each and every one of the outstanding pledges left owed to the clinic. And tonight, when he'd told her that if anyone was unkind to her they'd answer to him… The gravelly warning in his voice—for *her,* on *her* behalf—had touched her so deeply, her throat had momentarily closed. She'd never had a champion. She was so used to fighting her own battles, it had simply become second nature. And strictly speaking, she didn't need anyone to fight her battles for her, but it was nice to know that he cared enough to stand in the gap for her.

"I would have increased your budget, or helped solicit donations. Whatever would have made you happy," he'd said.

Her happiness, her feelings, what mattered to her.

She swallowed tightly. She could do a whole helluva lot worse than letting Robin Sherwood care for her. She'd do good to remember that.

Lord knows there were so many other things about him that she wasn't in danger of forgetting. The heat in that wicked hazel gaze when he looked at her, the angle of his head as he bent over her foot, the taste of his shoulder as he pistoned in and out of her, his warm, hard body surrounding hers as she convulsed around him, the look in his eyes as he laid her down on her bed—proprietary, victorious and endearingly uncertain. The exact curve of his best smile, the slightly lopsided grin that somehow managed to hook her heart and tug every time he aimed it at her.

A line emerged between her brows as a thought suddenly struck. "Right before you kissed me tonight, you asked me to forgive you," she said. "Forgive you for what?"

He chuckled softly, his fingers slipping idly down her arm. "For not having the patience to wait until I walked you to your door to kiss you," he said. "Believe it or not, I'd had good intentions. I was going to behave like a proper gentleman on our first proper date."

She laughed. "I guess that makes me a proper tramp, then, since I gave it up so quickly, huh?"

Gave it up, hell. She'd practically demanded it. *Do it, Robin, whatever you're thinking.* She'd known exactly what he was thinking—what he'd wanted—and knew that he'd been struggling with his conscience, trying to be considerate of her feelings. Little did he know that her feelings had mirrored his own and were equally depraved.

He turned and pressed a kiss to her temple. "Ha. Trust me, sweetheart. Nothing about getting you into bed has been easy. Hell, you didn't even want to let me into your house," he said, laughing softly. "I had little hope of ever making it into your bed. But I should warn you, now that I'm here, I won't be easily ejected."

She hugged him closer, nuzzled her nose against his chest and slipped a foot along his calf. "No worries, you're not in any imminent danger of that." She paused for a moment. "Can I ask you something?"

"Of course."

"Were you really okay with leaving the military?"

Though she hadn't notice a limp, the scars had been hard to miss. His right thigh was covered in them, angry red lines, puckered skin. If this was the result of healing, then she could only imagine what the original wound had looked like.

"I was surprised when I heard that you were coming home," she continued, feeling him still beneath her. "I figured you'd go into an instructor's position, perhaps take over some supersecret circle of specialized Rangers or something." He'd always been so proud of his military service, seeming to think it was the best way to honor his father's memory.

He released a small breath. "It took me a little while to get used to the idea," he admitted. His voice was measured, quiet, as though he hadn't talked about this before. "I'd built a family there—apart from John and his father, I mean," he added. "I appreciated the structure, the rules and regulations, the commitment to a common goal, a common good. I enjoyed the physical challenges and found the study of military tactics fascinating."

She was sensing a but…

"But war is hell, Marion. Death and destruction, broken bodies and buildings, ravaged land. I've lost more friends than I care to count." He paused, swallowed. "If a soldier ever tells you he's not afraid of dying, then that's the one person you don't want beside you. Because you *need* to be afraid, dammit—that fear is what keeps you alive."

Marion's heart squeezed, touched that he'd share this with her.

"After the hit to my thigh, when it became clear that I was no longer going to be able to do the job I'd been trained for, I decided it was time to come home. I wanted to put down some roots—my roots, in my own place," he said. "That was important. Everywhere I've ever lived has belonged to someone else—my grandfather, private schools, the military. I'd never had anything that was just mine." He chuckled uncertainly, as though he'd revealed too much, described a character flaw. "Does that make sense?"

Marion released a slow breath. "More than you can imagine," she told him. "How do you think I ended up here? I'd lived at the cottage on the estate, then in a college dorm, then with Mom until three years ago because she didn't want to be left alone. This was my first place and I was determined that it was going to be all mine, without thought or regard for anyone else who might ever live in it with me. That's why it's pink, that's why there's no spare room, that's why there's no double vanity. It's mine."

She felt him grin. "I did wonder about the pink," he admitted. "Such a girly color."

She laughed. "Newsflash—*I'm* a girl."

He reached over and slid a thumb over her nipple. "Believe me, sweetheart, I'm not in any danger of mistaking you for anything else."

A delicious shiver worked its way through her and she turned and kissed his chest, inched up, sliding deliberately toward his mouth. "Good to know."

He gave her a squeeze, drawing her more fully up against him, the hot hard length of him pressing against her. "Spend the day with me tomorrow," he said, his voice warm and low, rough with longing and something else. Uncertainty, maybe? "Come to the farm."

It was that hint of vulnerability that got her, Marion decided. The barest suggestion of insecurity, as if he was afraid of being rejected. It blew her mind that someone so confident, so self-assured could have any self-doubt. Such a dichotomy.

"Justine should be able to handle things for a day in my absence," she said, searching his gaze for more clues, more evidence of his thoughts.

Hope lit his eyes. "So you'll come?"

She nodded, slid a thumb over the sleek line of his brow and smiled. "I will."

He sighed, his chest deflating, his breath seeping into her mouth on a kiss, and it wasn't until that moment that she realized he'd been holding his breath.

Waiting for her answer.

She smothered a whimper. Sweet, dear man, Marion thought. Her poor heart never stood a chance.

He owned it. He always had.

9

"SERIOUSLY?" MARION WHEEDLED, her eyes wide. "You've just watched me eat the Trucker's Breakfast at Wilma's Chicken and Waffles and you're going to make me listen to 'Baby Got Back'?" She arched a dark brow. "Permission to change the radio station, Major?" she asked, leaning forward in anticipation.

Robin chuckled, impressed that she'd asked. Hell, he'd seen friends divorce over radio and thermostat arguments. "Go ahead," he said with a careless shrug, aiming the truck toward Mockingbird Road.

She scanned a few stations, skipping over various songs with a frown, until she happened upon Ed Sheeran's "Give Me Love." He nodded appreciatively and drummed a thumb against the steering wheel. Good choice.

The sky was a beautiful October blue, that bright otherworldly turquoise that only seemed to come in the fall. A rolling landscape of multicolored leaves painted both sides of the road as they drove farther and farther away from the city. There was distinct chill in the air this morning when they'd left for breakfast, a crispness that promised an even chillier evening. It was a good night for a fire, Robin thought, hoping that he could talk her into staying with him. She'd brought a bag with her and put out extra food and water for Angus, but he was trying not to read too much into her actions, afraid to get his hopes up.

He was relatively certain that he'd finally gotten through to her, that she was done running from him and would let *this*—whatever it was between them—play out the way it was meant to be.

This relationship had been twenty-five years in the making—he remembered when she was born, after all—and he wanted to grab hold of this opportunity and not let go.

Which pretty much summed up what he'd like to do with her, as well.

Honestly, when he'd awoke this morning, her delightful rump nestled against his groin, the pleasant weight of her ripe breast in his hand, the scent of her hair in his nose... He couldn't remember ever feeling so content, so certain that he was in the right place at the right time. He'd cast a rueful glance around her purple bedroom, at the fluffy pillows and floral prints and breakable things, and known with certainty that, if she asked, he'd live in that feminine fortress if it meant he could be with her.

But he'd keep his balls, thank you very much.

This was why he'd avoided her—because he'd known he'd want her—and, while he'd never doubted that she desired him, *wanting* him was another matter altogether.

It was galling, really—and humbling, if he was honest—to be so...unsure. He thought she cared about him, but he had so little experience with love and relationships, how was he to know? He knew *he'd* never felt this way before. He could only hope that she felt the same way about him. And if she didn't, then he'd figure out a way to make her.

Because she needed him as much as he needed her.

Other than Justine, the best he could tell, Marion was

every bit as isolated as he was. She'd mentioned last night that she hadn't seen or spoken to her father in years, that he'd left shortly after Michael's death. He'd known that, of course, but he'd never realized that the rift hadn't been repaired. As for her mother, she'd moved to North Carolina to live with her sister. Marion was careful about what she revealed about her mother, simply saying she was "remote."

No doubt *remote* meant she'd severed any parental obligation to her daughter. It made his blood boil. They'd lost Michael, but Marion had, too, and they still had another child to love and protect.

In his opinion, the pair of them had failed miserably.

He wanted to make up for that, wanted to be the person she could count on, that she could trust. He wanted to be her safe harbor in a storm, her retreat, her lover, her confidant and friend. He wanted to take care of her, not because she needed him to, but because she deserved it. She'd been taking care of everyone around her for years. Who had Marion's back? Who shored her up? Who could she turn to?

Him, Robin thought. If she'd let herself.

They still hadn't talked about Michael, but in reviewing the list Justine had given him—the one that cited all the people who benefitted from Marion's "discretionary fund"—he thought he'd worked out a solution to that, as well. One that would honor both her and her late brother.

Marion's cell phone chirped. She fished it out of her purse and looked at the display. Her eyes rounded, then watered, and a smile curled her lips.

"What?" he asked, concerned. "Is something wrong?"

She turned to look at him, her gaze soft with disbelief and gratitude. "Justine just sent me a text." She swallowed tightly, seemingly struggling to find her voice. "*Every* outstanding pledge has been honored this morning. Honored and doubled."

She launched herself at him, laughing delightedly, and rained kisses all over his cheek. "You did this," she said. "I don't know exactly how and I don't care, but I know that you did it." She drew back, stroked his cheek. "Thank you, Robin. We can do a lot of good with this money."

Not *I*, but *we*. His heart lightened. There was hope for them yet.

COTTONWOOD WAS EXACTLY AS Marion remembered it. The big white farmhouse sat deep in a grove of cottonwood trees, overlooking a large pond. Ducks and geese currently skimmed the surface, and Robin's cows bellowed from the pasture. The farm was peaceful, but alive with activity.

It was also surprisingly simple. The bulk of his furniture had been mined from antiques stores and an Amish community not far from where he lived. Lots of tall windows provided ample light, bathing the rooms in a golden glow. His kitchen had been outfitted with an old copper farmhouse sink—one she coveted—and copper ceiling tiles, which had been rescued from an old feed and seed store, covered the ceiling. It was big and livable and warm and the view from the front porch couldn't be beat.

"This is gorgeous, Robin," she said, watching his lips curl around the edges at her compliment. As though he were relieved.

"Thank you," he said. "I thought you'd like it. Other than John, you're only the only guest I've ever had."

She turned to look at him, irrationally pleased. "Really? I'm honored."

He slung an arm around her shoulders, then pulled her closer to him. "You're special, nitwit, or hadn't you figured that out yet?"

The bottom dropped out of her stomach, and pleasure bloomed through her. "Nitwit," she echoed. "Not exactly the endearment I would have chosen, but…"

His eyes twinkled. "What would you like me to call you?"

"Oh, I don't know. 'Goddess' has a nice ring to it."

A bark of laughter broke up from his throat. "Goddess, huh? You are that," he conceded. "My lady in red."

"You're really hung up on that cape, aren't you?"

"Did you bring it with you?"

She laughed. "Sorry, no."

He made a moue of regret. "No worries, I like your battle dress better anyway."

She blinked, confused. "My battle dress?"

He wrapped a tendril of her hair around his finger and gently pulled her to him, lowered his mouth to hers, brushing her lips, once, twice, three times. "Your beautiful, gloriously naked body," he explained, his voice husky. "*That's* your battle dress. The one guaranteed to win any war. I'm defenseless against it."

Sweet Lord, if he didn't stop saying things like that to her, she was going to start believing him. Her breath shallowed out as desire flooded her, making her breasts go heavy and ache, her womb swell with an itchy heat. She deepened the kiss, wrapped her arms around his powerful frame, his brilliantly sculpted body. His shoulders were a work of art, the perfect combination of sleek skin stretched over muscle and bone.

"You know what I just realized," he said, pulling her to him.

"What?"

He swept her up off her feet and headed for the door. "I haven't shown you the bedroom yet."

Marion giggled, licked a path along his neck and

breathed into his ear, gratified when he shivered. "That's awfully remiss of you."

"Making the correction now," he said as he negotiated the stairs. He carried her as though her weight were negligible—when it wasn't, she knew—without breaking stride or any heavy breathing. It was a romantic, caveman gesture and it thrilled her to her little toes. Marion vaguely noted the large four-poster bed before she landed against it, the mattress soft and pillowy at her back.

He was hard and firm at her front.

He looked down at her, his hazel gaze wicked, his smile rife with masculine satisfaction. "Do it," he told her. "Whatever you're thinking, do it."

She chuckled low, recognizing her own words. Then she deliberately rolled him over, sat back on her haunches and let her gaze travel slowly over him. "I'm going to go ahead and get into my battle dress," she murmured, whipping her sweater over her head.

His eyes glazed over and he waited with bated breath as she slowly unclasped her bra. She popped the front closure, allowing the fabric to sag. It clung to her nipples and with a slight shrug, she let it fall.

He gulped, his pupils dilating. His fingers clenched, but he held himself still, content to let her lead. She leaned back and unfastened her jeans, released the zipper, then took her time lowering them over her hips.

His breathing grew shallow and he licked his lips and swallowed, his eyes going a deep amber with desire. She loved the way he looked at her, the way his greedy gaze slid over her. It melted her bones, loosened her muscles. Made her nipples tingle, her sex simmer. She took as much time with her panties as she had her jeans and by the time she was fully undressed, his breathing was ragged.

"Marion," he choked desperately, "you're killing me."

"It's war," she said, smiling foggily, her fingers trailing over his chest. While she'd taken her time removing her own clothes, she didn't waste any removing his. She ripped his shirt off, buttons ricocheting to the floor.

He laughed brokenly, his eyes widening in shock. "I hated that shirt anyway," he said, letting a rough breath escape as her tongue touched his nipple. She ran her hands along each one of his ribs, playing them like a harp against her fingertips, then licked a path down his belly. She rubbed him through his jeans, feeling the hot, hard length of him jump against her palm, then she crouched between his legs. She lowered the zipper and he lifted his hips, helping her in the process. She looked up at him, flipped her hair over her shoulder so it wouldn't be in the way, then arched a brow, smiled and took him first in hand, then into her mouth.

He jerked, growled low and fisted his hands in the coverlet. *"Marion."*

She circled the engorged head with her tongue, licking him. "You said to do whatever I was thinking," she said, barely recognizing her own voice. Who was this woman? "I was thinking about doing this. About feeling this part of you in my mouth." She licked him again, suckled deep. "The soft parts," she murmured. Closed her lips over him once more, then relaxed her throat and ate the whole of him. "The hard parts."

Another desperate groan ripped from his throat, emboldening her further, giving her more confidence to wage this carnal war, to lay siege, to conquer. She massaged his tautened balls, then took him deep once more, sliding her tongue along from root to tip, savoring the taste of him against her mouth. His thighs were rigid, his hands convulsing, and a look at his face revealed a locked-tight jaw and eyes that were made with longing.

It was the eyes that got her, that propelled her forward. She scaled his magnificent body, straddled him, then sank slowly onto him, fully impaling herself. He growled, grabbing her hips and thrusting up into her. He bent forward and took a breast into his mouth, suckling hard, the same way she'd just done to him. Her clit tingled in response, as though an invisible thread connected one part of her to the other and she rode him harder, undulating her hips against him. She leaned back, taking more of him, and he came with her, his mouth everywhere. Her breasts, her chest, her neck. His big wonderful hands shaped her ass, squeezing her with every measured roll of her hips.

She caught that magical rhythm, the one that made her womb quicken, her breath come in quick, sharp little gasps and followed it until the orgasm crested, then broke in a rainbow of sensation so intense her vision blackened around the edges.

Robin bucked wildly beneath her, his lips peeled back away from his teeth, his eyes heavy-lidded, clouded with want. Harder, faster, then harder still and she absorbed the thrusts, her breasts bouncing on her chest. Three manic thrusts later, he roared, then went rigid beneath her. She could feel him pulsing deep inside of her, every explosive contraction of his release.

It was odd, that sensation, knowing that, had she not been on birth control, the seed she literally felt filling her body could have taken root and produced a little Robin. A little archer. A vision of this child, this tawny-haired version of Robin, made something in her throat tighten, made her feminine muscles contract, ostensibly to hold that part of him in, to encourage it to take root.

Shaken by the longing that suddenly welled up inside of her, Marion collapsed against his chest. His chest heaved beneath her, his fingers stroked her spine, then he picked up a corner of the white sheet and waved it awkwardly at her.

"I surrender," he said, chuckling breathlessly. "You win."

Yes, Marion thought, happiness and contentment washing through her, saturating every pore as she lay there with him, afternoon light spilling into the bedroom.

For the first time in her life, she believed in the victory.

10

"It's going well, then?" John asked. He inspected the fuse box, deemed it acceptable, then turned to Robin and waited for his answer.

"It is," he said.

"'Bout damned time," John said with a meaningful nod. "Honestly, it's like the blind leading the blind with you two."

"Yeah, yeah," Robin said, walking back into what would be the communal kitchen of the Maid Marion Safe House. "So what do you think?" he asked. "I called you down here to inspect the building, not critique my love life."

"If it wasn't for me, you wouldn't have a love life." He offered Robin an annoying smug look. "Have you forgotten the foot-kissing bet?"

"Have you forgotten you owe me two grand?" Robin replied.

John grinned. "The structure is sound. I can put a team on it and have the first three floors completely renovated within a month."

Robin winced. "I need it sooner," he said. "At least the kitchen and a single apartment." Gage, in all probability didn't have a month. The boy needed a safe place to go now, a clean place to lay his head, a stocked kitchen to put food in his belly. Out of all the people on Marion's personal list, Gage's situation was admittedly the most dire.

He'd finally drummed up the nerve to ask her about the boy last night. She hadn't been the least surprised that Justine had outed her. "She can't keep a secret," she'd complained with an eye roll. They'd laid on the braided rug in front of his fireplace last night and talked for hours, then made love, then slept. Seeing her hair spilled out on his pillow this morning had made him want to beat his chest and roar, a seemingly perpetual state of late.

She was lovely, his lady in red. A breathing angel.

John was thoughtful for a moment. "I'll fast-track it," he said. "In the interim, the boy can come and stay with me."

Robin blinked. "Stay with you?"

John shrugged. "I'm in the city. I'll get the kid a key and a cell phone, and he can stay with me when he wants to with the understanding that I need to know where he is. I won't put any demands on him, since it sounds like he's carrying a heavy enough load as it is."

Robin was speechless, evidently insultingly so to John, who suddenly glowered at him.

"Don't look so damned surprised," he said. "Hell, I'm not heartless. You haven't got the market cornered on good deeds."

"No, I—" He nodded, still at a loss. John Little didn't live a monastic life by any stretch of the imagination. He liked to drink, watch movies with tasteless humor and eat junk food.

Come to think of it, a teenager would probably be a good roommate for him.

Robin smiled at him. "It's a wonderful idea. Marion will be thrilled."

"Yes, she will," John said with a succinct nod. "And

that's all you care about, anyway, isn't? It's always been for her."

Robin stilled, frowning at him. "What do you mean?"

"The clinic," John told him, his gaze clear of all humor, of sentiment. "Admit it, Robin. It was never about Michael—it was about Marion. About keeping her close. About holding on to to her."

For reasons that escaped him, Robin's heart suddenly raced, and his mouth went dry, forcing him to swallow. "That's not fair," he said. "Michael was a friend."

"Yes, he was, but if I died tomorrow, would you found any kind of memorial in my honor?" He shook his head sadly, as if Robin was slow. "Not that I'd expect you to, of course. But you wouldn't."

"My family was at fault. My grandfather— We owed them—" He couldn't finish any argument because he knew none of them were valid. John was right, he thought, sagging with the realization.

It *had* been for Marion. For the very reasons his friend had pointed out.

John winced at him. "Ordinarily, you're a pretty sharp guy and you know I love you like a brother, so I'm going to tell you something that you should know, but probably don't believe yet."

Still shaken, Robin looked up at him.

"You are *nothing* like your grandfather and will never be in danger of becoming like him." He grinned suddenly. "You're your father's son, Robin. Gavin's. Not Henry's." He snorted. "Hell, I question if Gavin was even Henry's. There were rumors—" He stopped short and shook his head.

Robin's gaze sharpened. "Rumors? Rumors about what?"

John hesitated, shook his head. "I shouldn't have said anything."

"No," Robin said. "Whatever it is that you haven't told me should have been said a long time ago. What?" he persisted. "What rumors?"

John studied him for a long, considering moment. "My grandfather seemed to think that Henry was sterile. But rather than admit it and appear 'less of a man,' he blamed your grandmother. He'd told her that he picked her up out of the gutter and could put her back again if she didn't produce a child. The implication was that he didn't care how she gave him that child. And your dad bore a marked resemblance to a handsome Air Force pilot who was on the Atlanta scene in the early sixties." John paused. "Dad's got pictures of him."

Robin swallowed, stunned. "Why are you just telling me this now?"

"Because it's never been important before," John said. "I don't want you to make a mistake because of some misguided notion of 'bad blood.' Assuming that it's even true," he added. "It'll be up to you whether or not you investigate."

It would certainly explain a lot, Robin thought. The contempt, the apathy with which Henry treated him. His grandfather wanted an heir, not a son.

Robin didn't give a damn about an heir…but a son? A daughter? With Marion. His own family. It was a heady thought, one that took root and grew into a yearning he would have never expected so swiftly. They hadn't used any protection, though she'd mentioned that she was on birth control. Had it not been for that, she could be pregnant right now, her belly growing ripe with his seed.

"You okay?" John asked.

Robin shook himself. "Yeah, I'm fine," he said. "It's a lot to take in."

"Let me know if you want to see those pictures. You can decide for yourself if there's a resemblance."

"Thanks, I will."

John turned to leave and Robin stopped him.

"John?"

He paused and shot him a look.

Robin swallowed awkwardly, then grinned. "I would most definitely open some sort of memorial in your honor. Probably a hot dog stand or an ice cream truck," he added. "But something."

John grinned. "Name your firstborn after me," he said, feigning humility. "That's all I ask."

Robin laughed. "Sorry, Little Sherwood sounds like a tree."

"Smart-ass."

But John Gavin Sherwood had a nice ring to it.

And speaking of rings, he had an appointment with a jeweler. He wasn't wasting any more time. He wanted Marion. He wanted to marry her and have babies. He wanted to fight with her, then have make-up sex, then even more sex. He wanted to watch her blink the sleep from her eyes in the morning, listen to the even sound of her breathing as she slept beside him at night. He wanted to serve her breakfast in bed and buy her presents just because.

He just wanted her. And it was about time that he told her that.

JUSTINE BUZZED HER OFFICE. "Marion, Henry Sherwood is on line one," she said, her voice uncertain and curious.

Marion felt her eyes widen. Henry Sherwood? Why was he calling her? She hadn't heard from that old man in years, not since he'd personally walked through their cottage with them and deducted every door ding and bit of chipped paint—normal wear and tear on a place he'd never kept up—from her mother's last paycheck.

For one heart-stopping instant, she was afraid something had happened to Robin. But she quickly discarded that idea. It had been John who'd called when Robin had been injured in Iraq, not Henry. So what in the hell had prompted him to get in touch with her after all these years.

With a sense of resignation and dread, Marion finally decided she wasn't going to get the answers to that question without talking to him. She sighed, braced herself, then picked up the phone.

"Marion Cross."

"Cook's Daughter? Is that you?" the thin voice demanded.

Her teeth immediately went on edge. "This is Marion Cross, if that's who you're looking for."

He grunted. "I suppose it is," he said. "Do you know who this is?" he asked, as though she *should* know, a classic intimidation tactic.

She wasn't impressed and she wasn't an impressionable young girl anymore, either. She played dumb. "My secretary said you were Henry Sherwood. Is that not correct?"

"Yes, it is," he snapped. "You know what I mean."

"Is there something I can help you with, Mr. Sherwood? Do you need medical assistance?"

"I've got my own nurses," he bellowed. "I don't need your charity or that rag-tag team of so-called professionals you've got there on staff."

Marion stilled and bit the inside of her cheek until it hurt. "If there is a point to this call, Mr. Sherwood, then I suggest you make it. I'm busy."

"Fine," he snapped. "Stay the hell away from my grandson, Cook's Daughter. You're not our kind of people. You don't belong in our world."

The dart didn't penetrate, but stung all the same.

Furthermore, Marion didn't know what was more alarming, that he knew she'd been seeing Robin—no doubt the old man had been paying someone to watch his grandson and report back—or that he seriously thought she wanted to be part of "his" world. She knew she didn't belong in his world—there were very few people who did, thank God—but it annoyed her that she'd allowed him to undermine her sense of insecurity.

"You're opinion is noted and rejected. Now if that is all, I've got things I—"

"No, it's bloody well not all," he exploded. A variety of machines started going off, dinging in the background and she heard someone tell the old man that he had to calm down. "Don't touch me!" he yelled. "I'm fine, damn you!"

"Goodbye, Mr. Sherwood."

"I'll disinherit him," he shouted before she could disconnect.

Marion paused, stunned at the threat. "I won't leave him one red cent if he sees you again. He's the last of my line and this is his heritage. I won't see him flush it away on the help's daughter. Break it off with him," he said, gasping for breath. "Or on your head be it."

He hung up on her.

Justine stood in the doorway, her face a mask of concern. "What's wrong?" she asked. "You're white as a sheet. Is it Robin? Is he okay?"

Marion absently shook her head. "No, no, he's fine. It's nothing like that." She sat woodenly, shocked to the soles of her feet that anyone could be so manipulative, so evil. She told Justine what he'd said.

Her assistant's fake eyelashes rose to her eyebrows. "He

wouldn't do it," she said, her voice not as sure as the words she uttered. "Don't let that mean-spirited old bastard come between you and Robin. That boy is in love with you and has been for a long time," she said. She rolled her eyes. "Hell, you and him were the only ones who didn't know it. It was obvious to everyone else around here."

Robin was in love with her? Marion shook her head. "I don't think so, Justine. We've got a history, that's all."

"You've got more than a damned history—you've got chemistry. The very air vibrates around the two of you," she said, almost enviously. "And have you seen the way he looks at you? Like you're the sun and the moon and the stars all rolled into one?"

Did he look at her that way? Marion wondered. Could he really be in love with her?

Justine nodded knowingly. "Go ahead and doubt me," she said. "But that old bastard wouldn't have called here if he didn't believe it. Why would he, if you weren't a threat?"

Marion's heart galloped in her chest and her stomach dropped. Robin? In love with her? She knew he cared for her. After this past week, there was no denying that. She could feel it when he touched her, saw the stark longing in his gaze when he looked at her. But love?

"You love him, don't you?" Justine prodded, determined to excavate all of Marion's feelings.

"I—"

Justine stood abruptly, seemingly at her wit's end. "Oh, for the love of all that's holy. Admit it, would you! Just admit it! You love him. I know you love him, John knows you love him, all the nurse and doctors and patients here know you love him. You love him, Marion!"

"Yes!" she exploded. "Yes, of course I love him, dammit!" she cried, bolting from her chair, as well. "Who wouldn't love him? He's wonderful. He's good and decent and generous. He's clever and funny and hot," she added as an aside. "Have you seen that ass? Sweet heaven, it's a work of art."

"He's definitely got a fine ass," Justine concurred, her lips twitching with humor. She looked immensely proud of herself. She cleared her throat, then walked to the door, which had been left ajar. "By the way, Robin's here to see you," she said, ducking out quickly.

Marion gasped, belatedly realizing what her secretary had just done. Predictably, to her immense mortification, Robin appeared in the doorway, his hazel eyes twinkling with humor and satisfaction.

"You like my ass, huh?" he teased, the wretch.

"That's all you got out of that exchange?" she asked, her face flaming with embarrassment. There was no turning back now. It was out there. In the open. Her feelings. For him. There was no falling on her sword for his inheritance now, either. No doubt he'd heard all of that, as well.

He strolled forward, rounded her desk and sat on the edge next to her. "I might have heard you say that you loved me," he said, his sinfully sculpted mouth curled into that lopsided smile she loved. It was wicked, irreverent. Hot.

She swallowed, unable to look at him. He tipped her chin up with his finger, forcing her to meet his gaze. "They're all right, you know," he said. "I do love you. I always have. I don't know how I could have missed it, how I couldn't have known." A rueful smile tugged at his lips. "But sometimes it's the most obvious things that end up overlooked, right?"

Her eyes watered, emotion clogged her throat, and elation and despair simultaneously—impossibly—haunted her. "Oh, Robin, what are we going to do?" she asked hopelessly.

He reached into his pocket and withdrew a box, then carefully opened it, his big hands shaking slightly.

Oh! He wasn't— He couldn't— She gasped, covering her mouth with her hand.

"Well, I was kind of hoping we'd get married," he said. "It's about time, don't you think?" He grasped the ring—a vintage square-cut diamond in a simple platinum setting that was perfect, just perfect—and took her left hand in his. "What do you say, Marion? Do you want to spend the rest of your life with me? Will you let me love you? Let me make you happy?"

Tears streamed down her face and she shook all over. "Henry will disinherit you," she wailed. "You heard the call. He'll cut you off. You'll l-lose e-everything. And it'll be m-my f-fault."

He smiled indulgently at her, his heart in his eyes, the love she'd seen all along but never accepted reflecting back at her. "In the first place, that's not true. I've already inherited my father's portion, so that's not an issue. I'm in no danger of ruination, no matter what Henry says." He frowned. "And there's a very real possibility that Henry isn't really my grandfather, but that's a conversation for a different day."

She blinked drunkenly. "What?"

"The point is," he pressed, "that I would let it all go in a heartbeat because I'd be the poorest rich man on the planet without you, Marion. You're what matters, understand? Just you."

Justine heaved a huge, exasperated sigh from the hallway. "Marion, say yes," she wheedled. "Just say yes."

Robin grinned and shot a look toward the door. "I got this, Justine."

Marion sniffled. "My mother will flip out, "she warned him. "She'll be horrible."

He grinned, then chewed the inside of his cheek. "Do you really care?"

"Not in the least," she said, laughing through her tears. "But you've got to stop trying to pay for your grandfather's sins, Robin," she said. "What happened to Michael was awful, a tragedy. But it wasn't your fault." Her voice hardened. "And you're nothing like your grandfather."

"You're the second person to tell me that today," he told her.

"Who was the first?"

"John."

"Smart guy, John," she said, savoring the sight of him. Eating him up with her gaze. *Let me love you. Let me make you happy.* Her head spun merrily.

"He wants us to name our firstborn after him."

She laughed and rolled her eyes. "He would."

He squeezed her hand. "You still haven't answered me, Marion."

She peeked up at him beneath lowered lashes. "Ask me again. I want to do this right."

"Tell me you love me," he said. "I heard it, but you didn't say it to me."

She reached up and cupped his cheek, tracing his dear face with her fingers. "I love you, Robin. Always. You really didn't know, did you?"

"I'd begun to hope," he said with a small shrug. His gaze tangled with hers once more and the love and affection she saw in those hazel eyes would have sent her to her knees if she hadn't already been sitting down. "Marry me, Marion," he breathed. "Be my bride."

"I will," she said, laughing happily as he slid the ring onto her finger. She wrapped her arms around him, holding him close as happiness blazed through her. "You were right," she said.

"I usually am," he teased. "You should file that away for future reference. I suspect it'll come in handy."

She rolled her eyes, framed his face with her hands and kissed him.

He drew back. "For the sake of argument, though, what was I right about this time?"

Her eyes twinkled. "You are stubborn."

A dark chuckle rose from his throat, and he lifted his shoulders in a helpless shrug. "I warned you."

She grinned. That he did.

Epilogue

Nine months later...

JOHN SLUNG AN ARM AROUND Gage's shoulder and nodded significantly at the baby currently nestled in Robin's arms. "Proof positive that birth control isn't infallible," he told him. "Remember that, my man."

Gage blushed to the roots of his hair and grinned.

Marion gasped in outrage. "John, that's inappropriate," she scolded. She looked at Robin and gestured toward their guests. "Robin, say something. Can't you do anything about him?"

Robin merely grinned innocently. "I've never been able to in the past," he said. "I don't know why you think he'd start listening to me now."

Truthfully, he didn't think he needed to interfere with John and Gage at all. What had begun as a simple solution to a big problem had morphed into a bond between the two that no one had expected. Gage respected John, honored his rules and trusted him. And John clearly adored the boy. It was a bro-mance made in heaven. When Gage's mother had passed away, the boy had moved in permanently with

John. He was enrolled in school, in honor's classes, no less, and finally had a little meat on his bones.

Robin had given his wife the Maid Marion Safe House as a wedding present. She'd turned the running of the clinic over to Justine and had taken over the Safe House herself. The house was more than a bed—it was an apartment, a fixed space for residents—with a community kitchen that was always open, a big great room with lots of seating. There was also a library and a computer lab, and Marion arranged to have different skilled education classes on site on a regular basis. She was a wonder, his wife, and the residents adored her.

As they should, because she was perfect.

For him, anyway.

Despite his earlier opinion about men and pink houses, he'd offered to move in with her and give up Cottonwood so that she could be closer to the safe house, but once they'd realized a baby was imminent, she'd said the farm was the best place to raise a family.

Henry Sherwood, despite his threat, hadn't disinherited Robin when he'd married Marion, and the full scope of his fortune was left to Robin upon his death. They sold the estate and split the money between the clinic and the safe house.

A blood test confirmed that Henry *wasn't* Robin's biological grandfather.

After additional investigation, neither was the Air Force pilot.

The secret of whoever had fathered Robin's dad had evidently gone to the grave with his grandmother.

And, more than likely, with his grandfather, as well.

As Marion had predicted, her mother hadn't approved of their relationship. Though they'd invited her to the wedding, the invitation went unanswered and she didn't attend. While admittedly it had disappointed her, Marion knew that she'd done her part to repair the relationship and her mother simply hadn't wanted to heal the breach. So she and Robin moved forward, determined to build their own family.

His gaze dropped to the tiny bundle currently resting in his arms and a lump lodged in his throat. *His* child. *Their* baby. His chest ached with happiness.

"Well?" John asked, smiling hopefully. "What's the verdict? What have you decided to name the little one?"

Robin and Marion shared a significant look, hesitated, then Robin walked over and put the baby in John's big arms. His oldest and dearest friend—his brother from another mother, they liked to joke—laughed nervously, a wondering smile sliding over his face. "Meet John Michael Gavin Sherwood," Robin told him. "You'll be godfather, of course."

John's eyes moistened and he nodded. "I'd be honored," he said, his voice thick.

JOHN SHERWOOD HAD THE TAWNY curls of his father, the ice-blue eyes of his mother and was better with a bow and arrow than anyone in the state of Georgia.

And, as Robin predicted, Marion never lost an argument once she donned her battle dress.

* * * * *

KAREN FOLEY

GOD'S GIFT TO WOMEN

For Brenda Chin.
Thank you for your insight, your support and your talent for turning rough stones into polished gems!

1

Lexi Adams tried to ignore the sound of hammering from outside her bedroom window, wanting only to go back to the sensual dream she'd been having. She groaned and bunched her pillow around her head, but the incessant racket continued. Cracking an eyelid, she lifted the pillow enough to peer groggily at the bedside clock, certain it was still the middle of the night. But no, it was eight o'clock. On a Sunday morning.

Whack! Whack!

Pushing herself to a sitting position, Lexi blew a tendril of hair out of her face and yawned hugely. Obviously, she wasn't going to sleep late this morning. Swinging her legs to the floor, she padded across the room to the window and raised the shade, squinting at the bright sunlight. The arts-and-crafts-style bungalow next door had been empty for nearly a year, but the for sale sign on the front lawn had vanished the week before. From the sound of it, the new owner had sent a construction crew over to do some repairs. But really? On a Sunday morning? Was nothing sacred anymore?

A tall plank fence separated the two properties, but from her bedroom window, Lexi had an unobstructed view of the house and the backyard, which boasted a gorgeous in-ground swimming pool and cabana. Of course, the pool was empty and the lawn was mostly weeds, but with some attention, the house really had great potential. And the view was spectacular, situated as it was on a steep hill overlooking Santa Barbara, with the blue waters of the Pacific shimmering in the distance.

A movement behind the house, combined with the sound of renewed hammering, caught her attention and Lexi leaned forward for a better look. The back of the house was cast in shadows and partially hidden by an overgrown shrub, but she could just make out a ladder leaning against the wall, and the figure of a man standing high on the rungs. As she watched, he stepped down and away from the ladder to survey his work.

Lexi's mouth went dry.

He was shirtless, and a leather tool belt hung low on his hips. His tawny skin gleamed under a light sheen of sweat, throwing his muscles into sharp relief. She couldn't recall the last time she'd seen such a magnificent body and she strained for a better look. The brim of a black baseball cap shadowed his features, but his jaw might have been chiseled from stone. Lexi watched, entranced, as he dipped his hand into the front pouch of his tool belt for a handful of nails, and mounted the ladder once more.

"No, no," she murmured in protest as he disappeared behind the shrub.

Feeling a little foolish, she darted into the adjoining bathroom where a small window afforded her a better view. She devoured him with her eyes. Physically, he was the most amazingly perfect man she had ever seen, and she was certain that his sculpted body was the result of raw, hard work and not a regimen of fitness-center workouts.

Every muscle and sinew in his powerful shoulders and

arms flexed as he pounded a section of board into place. His jeans were faded and paint-spattered, but hugged his trim butt and thighs so perfectly that Lexi leaned against the window frame and sighed in appreciation. Her gaze traced the contour of his spine, admiring the play of muscles in his back and along his ribs. She could almost feel the warm, smooth texture of his skin, and her fingers curled into her palms.

Aware of the calluses there, she opened her hands and studied them. For the past two months, she had been working on a classical-Greek sculpture, commissioned by the Santa Barbara Art Association. Despite the fact she had submitted several preliminary mock-ups for the piece, she wasn't feeling the same inspiration that she had for her last project. The classical sculpture of Poseidon that she had completed six months earlier stood nearly thirteen feet high and would soon grace the new fountain at the Santa Barbara Botanic Gardens. She'd been enlisted to create a series of Greek sculptures as part of the new Garden of the Gods exhibit, and was looking forward to this latest project, a statue of Adonis. So maybe he wasn't exactly a god, but as far as Lexi was concerned, he was pretty close, and the art association had agreed to let her sculpt him. She had finished several clay busts and two scaled-down models. She'd also roughed out the figure on an eight-foot-high chunk of marble, but she wasn't satisfied. She admitted that she'd hit a stone wall. Literally. No matter how she tried, she couldn't envision the final work. The sculpture's face and physical attributes eluded her.

But looking at the gorgeous specimen next door, she realized she'd found her muse. Her hands itched to explore his contours. She could easily envision him nude. His buttocks would be firm and strong and his thighs corded with muscles. And his manly parts would be…manly.

She still hadn't seen his face, but it really didn't matter what he looked like. The advantage of being an artist was having the opportunity to create whatever she could imagine. And yes, she wanted to sculpt him. She *needed* to sculpt him. She suddenly knew that this stranger was the elusive image of Adonis that she had been searching for. Beauty like his was made to be admired, and she was convinced she could capture the essence of him.

Her own reaction to the man surprised her. After watching him for just ten minutes, she was already contemplating how she would refine the roughed-out marble in her studio. The stone would polish well, and she needed to provide an excellent finish in order to do justice to those gleaming muscles. Her classical sculpture of Poseidon had taken over a year to complete, but with the majority of the hard work on Adonis already done, it wouldn't take her long to fully release him from his marble enclosure, especially when she felt so energized. That's what surprised her most as she watched the man next door—how invigorated she felt.

Excitement surged through her as she watched the sexy stranger—the same thrill of anticipation that she always experienced when she embarked on a new project. She told herself that the sensation had everything to do with creative inspiration and nothing to do with the man as a person.

Absolutely nothing.

The very idea made her scoff softly, even as she craned her head through the window for a better look at his backside. Nope, she'd sworn off men more than six months ago, after her last relationship had ended in disaster. She had no interest in the opposite sex other than as subjects for her artistic interpretation. To be honest, she had yet to meet a man who could equal the qualities found in any of her sculptures. As conceited as it might sound, no man could measure up to her marble creations. So while she could appreciate this guy's physical attributes, she had no desire to get to know him on a personal level. Which meant that walking over and asking him to pose for her was out of the question.

"My camera," she breathed in a flash of insight, and padded quickly back into the bedroom and looked frantically around. Where had she left it? There. On the dresser. Grabbing the digital camera, she returned to the bedroom window, but couldn't get a clear shot of him through the panes. In frustration, she wrenched the window open and leaned out, quickly snapping off several frames of his broad shoulders and back. She preferred to use live models when creating her sculptures, but she could work from a photograph if she absolutely had to.

He climbed several more rungs and the shrubs obscured her view. Lexi was forced to lean farther out until her entire upper body stretched beyond the window frame. But she was unprepared when two more workers came around the corner of the house, one carrying a power saw and the second carrying lumber, which he set down across two sawhorses. The sexy stranger descended the ladder and turned in her direction. Swiftly, she snapped several more photos in quick succession and tried to duck back into the bathroom before he spotted her, but only succeeded in whacking the back of her head on the window sash.

She gave a sharp cry of pain and the camera slipped from her fingers and fell into the dense bushes that separated the two properties. Damn! She pulled herself inside the window, but not before the man lifted his head and looked directly at her. Their gazes collided, and for an instant, Lexi's heart stopped beating. With his face tipped up, she could see his features clearly beneath the brim of the baseball cap, and her eyes widened in dismay. Sweet mercy! Had she really thought it didn't matter what he looked like?

The man was a god.

In that brief instant, Lexi was aware that he did indeed have a jaw that might have been chiseled from stone, but his mouth had been fashioned purely from sin. She had a vague impression of haughty cheekbones, a proud nose and unusually light-colored eyes that expressed both surprise and annoyance before she recovered her wits and flattened herself against the inside wall, out of sight. Her heart hammered inside her rib cage and she pressed a hand against her chest in an effort to calm herself.

But the memory of his face wouldn't recede. And it wasn't just his face that had been unforgettable; she could still picture those perfect pecs and that cobblestoned abdomen, not to mention the deep, V-shaped groove that extended from his hip bones to beneath the low-slung waistband of his jeans. Every inch of the guy had been layered in sleek muscle.

Gathering her nerve, Lexi peeked around the edge of the window to the neighboring house, but while the other two men measured the lumber and quickly cut it with the power saw, her gorgeous stranger was no longer in sight. Relieved, she closed the window and dragged the shade down and then stared at her hands in dismay. They were trembling. She told herself that it had to do with the embarrassment of being caught hanging out a window, ogling a stranger, but the explanation seemed as shaky as her hands. The truth was, her composure had been rattled by those eyes. Less than five minutes ago, she'd viewed him only as a subject for her next sculpture. Then he had looked at her, and all she could think about was what it would be like to wrap herself around him.

She sucked in a deep breath and let it out slowly, silently acknowledging that with just one glance, he'd reduced her to a pile of quivering mush.

She didn't think he'd seen her actually taking pictures of him, thank goodness. Now she needed to retrieve her camera. Not taking the time to get dressed, Lexi slipped her feet into a pair of sandals and let herself silently out the back door.

The morning air was cool and fragrant with bougainvillea, and the day promised to be beautiful. Beyond the plank fence that separated the properties, she could hear the sound of renewed hammering. She walked quickly across the yard until she reached the narrow space between her house and the fence, where she had dropped her camera. She had to push her way into the dense shrubbery, swearing softly as the branches snagged her hair and scratched her exposed skin. Bending down, she peered through the foliage. She hoped that the thick vegetation had broken the camera's fall and protected it from serious damage.

The hammering from next door abruptly stopped. Lexi inspected the ground beneath the shrubs, but there was no sign of the camera. She was directly beneath the second-story bathroom window, so it had to be somewhere close by. Crouching down, she let her hand grope along the ground at the base of the shrub, her fingers searching blindly.

"Are you looking for this?"

The masculine voice startled Lexi so much that she jumped up, becoming tangled in branches and leaves. Shoving them aside, she peered through the foliage to see the stranger from next door leaning on the top of the fence. Her camera dangled from his fingers. Up close, he was breathtaking, with chiseled cheekbones and a wide, sensuous mouth. His eyes were a light shade of green, as pure and clear as the waters of the Mediterranean. His lashes were thick and sooty black, making the lightness of his eyes all the more dramatic. Right now, they were coolly amused as they assessed her.

"This was caught in the branches at the top of the bush," he said drily. "I only noticed because the sun reflected off the lens."

His voice was deep and smooth, and he spoke with an accent that Lexi found incredibly sexy. Now he studied the camera, and as she watched, he flicked it on and scrolled through the photos she had taken of him. His mouth pursed, either in consideration or disapproval, before he turned it off. The lens retracted with a soft whir.

"You can have your camera," he said quietly, shifting his attention back to her, "when you come over and ask me for it. I'd like to know why you were taking photos of me without my permission."

Mortified and more than a little dumbstruck by his looks, Lexi could only stare at him. "Okay." She nodded, her voice breathless. "Thank you."

One eyebrow went up, and Lexi wasn't sure, but she thought she detected a hint of a dimple in his cheek before he stepped down and disappeared. Lexi sagged against the shingles of the house, her heart racing.

Had she really just thanked him for confiscating her camera? She groaned. He probably thought she was a moron. She was a moron! She should have insisted that he return the camera right then, but now it seemed she would have to go next door and face him if she wanted to get it back. Just the memory of his eyes, filled with disapproval, made her cringe. It was as if he could see right into her. There was no way she could face him.

As she pushed free of the shrubbery, she decided he

could keep the camera. She'd rather give it up than suffer his censure. There had been something in his eyes that made her regret having taken the photos; something more than just disapproval.

Something like disappointment.

With a mental shake, Lexi told herself to forget it. To forget *him.* She had no interest in seeing him, or talking to him, or getting to know him on any level.

Even if he was perfect.

2

LEXI STOOD ON THE GRAVEL PATH at the Santa Barbara Botanic Gardens and watched as the flatbed truck backed slowly across the grass toward the fountain, emitting a series of strident warning beeps as it approached. The fountain was empty of water, and in the center stood a low, wide pedestal of white marble. On the back of the flatbed, secured with nylon tie-downs, stood her sculpture of Poseidon in all his bathysmal magnificence.

"He really is fabulous," enthused her friend, Nelda Denali, who owned an art gallery in downtown Santa Barbara. "I've become so accustomed to seeing him in your studio that it seems strange to think this will be his new home. By the way, I have the spare key you loaned me."

Lexi gave her friend a tolerant smile. "Keep it. We both know you're going to show up at the studio, wanting to store some overflow item."

Nelda winced, but Lexi saw the relief in her eyes. "You don't mind?"

"Of course not. It's a huge studio, bigger than I really need for just myself. I told you to feel free to use it for your extra pieces, and I meant it."

Nelda gave her a hug, and then looked around them at

the assembled group of people. "You have a good turnout for his christening."

Lexi had kept the sculpture in her studio for the past several months while the fountain was completed, and now the director of the botanic gardens, as well as several local dignitaries and members of the media, watched the workers prepare to transfer Poseidon to his new home.

"Well, now you can visit him anytime you want," Lexi assured her, snapping several photos of the sculpture. Half a dozen harnesses had been secured around the figure in preparation for lifting him onto the pedestal in the center of the fountain.

"Why are you using a dime-store disposable camera?" Nelda asked, watching as Lexi fiddled with the settings.

Lexi shrugged. "Because I accidentally dropped my good one out of a second-story window."

Nelda gasped. "You just bought that camera, and you paid a fortune for it! I hope you purchased an extra warranty."

They moved aside as the truck stopped at the edge of the fountain.

"The camera is fine, but it's been confiscated."

Nelda gave her a curious look. "What do you mean?"

As the workers secured the hoists, Lexi quickly related the story of how she'd been caught taking pictures of the man next door, and his conditions for returning the camera.

"You were taking pictures of him?" Nelda asked in astonishment. "Wow. He must really be something."

"You have no idea," Lexi said. "This guy is simply amazing. I've never met anyone like him. He's absolutely the most beautiful man I've ever seen. I want to sculpt him."

Her hands flexed as she spoke, as if in anticipation.

Nelda smirked. "Is that all you want to do with him?

Sounds as if you can't wait to get your hands on him for other reasons."

"Don't be ridiculous," Lexi scoffed. "The last thing I need is to get involved with some guy I don't know anything about. He's part of a construction crew hired to make repairs on the house next door. I'm not even sure he's American. Did I tell you he has an accent? I can't quite place it, but it's crazy sexy."

"So you want to sculpt him, but you don't want to get to know him." Nelda gave her friend a tolerant look. "You're like a modern-day female Pygmalion, more attached to your stone-cold sculptures than you are to real, warm-blooded men. Let me know how that works for you."

Lexi sighed, wondering if Nelda was right. Since her breakup with Ethan, she hadn't really been interested in getting involved with anyone. Until she'd seen the guy next door, nobody had excited her enough to make the effort.

"I'm not looking for a relationship right now," she said. "I have four more sculptures to complete for the gardens. My work is going to keep me too busy for anything else."

Nelda made a sound that clearly said she was unimpressed. "So you took some photos of this guy, but now he has your camera and won't return it until you ask him for it. So instead of trying to work from photos that you no longer have, why don't you walk over and just tell him that you're an artist and see if he'll agree to sit for you?"

Lexi chewed her lower lip. "I don't know…there's something about him. He makes me nervous."

"In a creepy way?"

Lexi grimaced. "No, just the opposite. In a pulse-racing, knee-quaking, he's-too-beautiful-for-me way."

Nelda stared at Lexi, her mouth open. "Are you kidding me? Have you looked in a mirror lately? I'd kill for your hair, not to mention your legs. Any guy would be lucky to have you take a second look at him, and I don't care how gorgeous he is."

Lexi laughed, and they stood silently for a moment as Poseidon slowly rose through the air, supported by three steel cables and guided by the hands of six workers. He floated over the fountain, and then descended until he stood in the center of the pedestal. Ensuring that the statue was level, the workers bolted it into place.

Lexi watched as the director of the gardens gave the order to turn on the water. Once the fountain was filled, the jets came to life and Poseidon seemed to rise from the spray. The garden-oversight committee had arranged for champagne to celebrate the event, and Lexi raised her glass in a toast, feeling a sense of pride and relief that everything had gone smoothly.

"Well, that's another successful project under your belt," Nelda said after Lexi shook hands with the director of the gardens and snapped a few final pictures of Poseidon. "What are you working on next?"

"I've been struggling with a sculpture of Adonis," Lexi confessed as they walked back toward the parking lot. "I mean really struggling. I just couldn't seem to envision the finished project." She paused. "Then I saw the guy next door, and suddenly he's all I can think about. He's exactly what I had in mind for Adonis, which is why I took the photos. I tried to sketch him from memory, but I just can't seem to capture him."

"Was he angry that you took his photos?"

Lexi considered the question for a moment. "No, not angry, exactly. He looked more disappointed than anything. Sort of resigned, you know? He probably has tons of people trying to take his picture. I'm sure it gets old after a while."

Nelda looked skeptical. "Really? He's that good-looking?"

"You have no idea." Lexi sighed.

"Okay, if you don't go over and get your camera, then I'm going to do it for you," Nelda declared. "I have got to see this man for myself."

Lexi pulled herself out of her reverie, knowing Nelda would do exactly as she said. "No! Please don't. I promise that I'll get my camera from him."

"And what are you going to say when he asks why you were snapping his picture?"

Lexi shrugged. "I'll tell him the truth, like you suggested—that I'm an artist and I want to sculpt him."

"Good," said Nelda approvingly. "If he's a laborer, then he might not make much money. Men are pretty simple creatures. I'm sure a little flattery and the promise of some extra cash will be enough incentive to model for you. But if I were you, I'd wear something hot, and it wouldn't hurt to bring some food with you. Guys love good food."

Lexi stared blankly at her. "Wear something hot? Are you kidding?"

"It couldn't hurt. You must have some sexy little dress that shows your cleavage and your legs. He won't be able to resist you."

"I'm not interested in sleeping with him, Nelda, just in sculpting him," Lexi said indignantly, but her words lacked the ring of sincerity.

"Yeah, right," Nelda scoffed. "At least if you're sleeping with him, you'll have easy access to his body for your sculpture."

Both women were silent for a moment as they considered this.

"I can put together a pretty decent picnic basket," Lexi mused.

NIKOS CHRISTAKOS STOOD AT THE kitchen sink washing the paint from a paintbrush when a movement outside caught his attention. He paused and watched through the window as the woman from the house next door made her way along the sidewalk to his front walk. Three days had passed since he'd caught her taking pictures of him, and he'd begun to think she wouldn't come over to claim her camera. He'd actually decided to head over and return it to her before he left for the day. Now he swiped his hands on a rag and leaned a hip against the counter to watch her approach.

She had a luminous beauty that had nothing to do with cosmetics or artificial enhancements. She wore a red flowered sundress that hugged her breasts and floated around her slender legs, and she carried a covered basket over one arm. Her dark hair hung in loose waves around her shoulders, and Nikos thought she resembled his fantasy version of Little Red Riding Hood. If that made him the Big Bad Wolf, he looked forward to gobbling her up.

Her stride was purposeful, causing her breasts to bounce gently with each step. Her expression was very serious, although he didn't miss how she opened and closed her hands several times as she walked. He finished wiping the paint from his hands as she began to knock, tentatively at first and then louder. His footsteps echoed through the empty house as he strode to the front door and pulled it open. She stood on the porch, hand poised to knock, and gaped at him.

"Oh!" She lowered her arm and then extended the basket to him with both hands. "Hi. I've come with a peace offering."

She was even prettier up close, and he thought he saw a mixture of apprehension and anticipation in her dark eyes. He could see she was nervous and he took pity on her. Opening the door wider, he stepped back.

"Come on in," he invited. Sensing her hesitation, he left the door open and turned to walk back through the hallway toward the kitchen. "Your camera is in here," he called to her over his shoulder.

He picked it up where he had left it and scrolled once more through the photos she had taken of him. When he glanced up, he saw she had stopped in the doorway of the kitchen. She held the basket in front of her like a shield, but her eyes were riveted on him as he held her camera.

He was struck again by her unusual looks. Despite her dark hair and eyes, her skin was so pale that it was almost translucent, as if she didn't get outside very often. But her shoulders and bare arms were toned and supple, evidence that she wasn't as fragile as she appeared. Nikos found the thought intriguing.

She came into the kitchen and set the basket down on the counter beside him, eyeing the camera. "I brought you some lunch," she said, opening the basket and tipping it toward him. "Some cheese and fruit, Caprese sandwiches, two bottles of sparkling water, and my own favorite—chocolate mousse. There's enough here for you and the rest of your crew."

Nikos glanced from the basket to her, and his mouth began to water. He told himself his sudden appetite was strictly for the food she had packed for him, and not the result of how delicious she looked in her red dress. He'd only had time for a cup of coffee that morning, and seeing the gourmet cheeses and crunchy bread reminded him of how hungry he was. She must want her camera back very badly if she had gone to the trouble of packing such an elegant meal for a bunch of construction workers.

"Are you trying to bribe me?" he asked, amused. He'd

meant it as a joke, but her eyes widened, and she snapped the basket closed.

"No! Of course not. I was just trying to be nice. I mean…" She stared at him as he raised an eyebrow, and her shoulders sagged. "Okay, yes. I'm totally trying to bribe you. I'm sorry I took pictures of you without your permission, but I really need my camera back. Please."

Nikos felt something tighten in his chest, and he wondered if she had any clue how charming she looked in her earnestness. He held her camera out to her. "Apology accepted."

She took the camera, her expression one of surprise. "That's it? You don't want to know why I took the pictures?"

A grin pulled Nikos's mouth. "Okay, I'm listening. Tell me why you took them."

"Well, I'm an artist, and—" She broke off with a self-conscious laugh. "This is going to sound so ridiculous."

"Try me."

She raised dark eyes to his, and Nikos felt a sudden tug of awareness, like the suck of an undertow pulling him helplessly out beyond his depth.

"You must know that you have an amazing physique. I can't remember the last time I saw—" She broke off again, and color stained her neck and face, vivid against her pale skin. Drawing a deep breath, she raised her chin. "I want to ask if you would be willing to model for me." She waited, expectant.

Now it was Nikos's turn to be surprised. It had been years since anyone had asked him to model for them. He wasn't naive enough not to be aware that he attracted a fair share of female attention, but he couldn't recall the last time a woman had commented so candidly on his appearance without even knowing him. Most women waited until they were in the bedroom to gush over his body. Although he knew he should enjoy the attention, he actually found it a little annoying. Did she realize that he had once been a top model in Europe? Or that he had abruptly left the business more than eight years ago? He no longer identified with that person. These days, he was simply a carpenter, and that's how he preferred to be known. He had no desire to step back in front of a camera.

"Sorry," he said. "I don't think so. But thank you for asking. I'm flattered."

Her eyes narrowed slightly, but he could see from the set of her chin that she was undeterred. "I would pay you, of course, and I could accommodate your schedule, although I work best in daylight. Perhaps if I spoke with your boss, he would agree to let you work part of the day here, and the remaining part with me. I—I would make it worth your while."

Nikos stared at her, his rampant imagination conjuring up decadent images of her. They were almost enough to make him agree to her proposal. When he finally found his voice, it sounded hoarse. "How?"

She looked a little panic stricken, as if she suddenly realized just how provocative her promise sounded. "Well," she said, floundering, "I could cover your wages for the time lost on this job, as well as pay you my standard sitting fee. In fact, I'll pay you ten percent more than what I normally give my models. And I would include meals."

Nikos experienced a mixture of disappointment and grudging admiration that she hadn't offered to have sex with him in return for his services. Not that he would have accepted such an arrangement. But for a brief instant, he allowed himself to imagine it. Immediately, heat gathered and spread through his body and he had to push the erotic thoughts out of his head.

"I'm sorry," he repeated, softening his rejection with a lopsided grin. "I'm pretty busy with this job, and I don't have a lot of extra time."

"Right. I understand." She looked regretful as she turned the camera over in her hands, then determinedly raised her chin and smiled. "Well, if there's anything I can do to change your mind…"

More images of her, delicately pale and gloriously nude, her dark hair spread across his bed, flashed through his head. He was an idiot to refuse her.

"Sorry."

She sighed and nodded. "Right. Well, enjoy the food." She held the camera up. "Thanks for this. I won't bother you again."

She turned to go, and Nikos didn't miss the defeated slump of her shoulders. He told himself that he had no cause to feel guilty for not accepting her offer. He had his reasons. He owed her nothing. But suddenly, he didn't want her to leave. Not like this.

"I'm working alone today," he said on impulse. "Why don't you stay and have lunch with me."

She turned back to him, eyes flitting between him and the basket of food, and then around the empty kitchen as if she suspected him of trying to trick her.

He gave her his most charming grin. "It'll just go to waste otherwise."

"Well, if you're sure…"

"I insist," he said, and moved to scoop up the basket before she could change her mind. "Let's take it outside."

Without waiting to see if she followed him, he moved through the empty house to the back door. After a moment, he heard her footsteps behind him. He held the door open for her and then led her through the construction debris in the backyard to a small table situated on the flagstones beside the empty pool. He set the picnic basket down on the table. Several small trees provided just enough shade that the sun didn't beat down on them. Eyeing her bare shoulders, he suspected she would burn easily.

"How is this?" he asked as she came to stand beside him.

"Perfect," she breathed, looking out over Santa Barbara to the distant blue of the Pacific Ocean. "No matter how many times I see this view, I never get tired of it."

"Yes, it's stunning," he said, letting his gaze drift over her features as he drew a chair out for her.

She glanced at him, uncertain, and then sat down, allowing him to adjust the chair beneath her. "What are you doing to the house, exactly?"

"My specialty is restoring older homes, like this one, to their original condition."

"Oh. I thought—" She broke off and gave an embarrassed laugh. "Well, never mind what I thought. I'm happy to meet you." She extended a hand toward him. "I'm Lexi Adams."

Her hand was slim and cool in his, but her handshake was strong. "Nikos Christakos," he said smoothly.

She stared at him with renewed intensity as he rounded the table and sat down across from her. "You're Greek."

"Yes." He opened the basket and began withdrawing the items inside. She had thought of everything, including glasses and wedges of lemon for the water. He pulled out several plates and set them down.

"I couldn't quite place your accent," she said, leaning forward to help him. "Which part of Greece are you from?"

Nikos sat back and watched as she poured two glasses of the sparkling water and then squeezed a wedge of lemon into each.

"I was born on the island of Syros, in the Aegean," he

replied, unwrapping two sandwiches and inhaling the fragrant aroma of fresh basil. Reaching over, he placed one sandwich on her plate. “Do you know it?”

Lexi shook her head. “No. I’ve always wanted to visit the island of Santorini, but I’ve never had the chance. I’ve heard it’s absolutely beautiful.”

“Oh, it is,” he assured her. “Santorini is part of the group of islands I grew up on.”

Lexi picked up her drink. “Wow. I bet that was amazing. The Greek Islands are my idea of paradise. Do you go back often?”

Nikos gave her a brief smile. “No. I left Syros when I was fourteen and I never returned. Someone once said that you can’t go home again, and it seems in my case, it’s true.”

3

LEXI STARED AT NIKOS, the underlying bitterness in his voice momentarily putting her at a loss for words. She didn't dare ask him why he had left. She told herself she didn't want to know.

Unsettled, she fussed with her meal, selecting several bits of fruit and cheese as she watched him furtively. He gazed out toward the ocean, his eyes distant and thoughtful. A breeze ruffled his hair, picking out the gold highlights in the darker brown strands. His eyebrows had drawn together, as if he was remembering something unpleasant, and Lexi had an almost irresistible urge to reach over and smooth the furrows from his brow.

Then he flexed his shoulders as if to shrug off the unwelcome thoughts, and turned to her with a smile. Lexi felt her breath catch in her throat at the sheer splendor of the man. He was male perfection, and in that instant she knew how she wanted to sculpt him.

Not Adonis; she wouldn't sculpt him as the embodiment of beauty and desire. He was so much more than that. She would portray him as Apollo, the Greek god of the sun. She hadn't yet begun to carve the details on the roughed-out sculpture that stood in her studio, so it wasn't too late to change direction. She could picture it clearly; a sculpture of the nude sun god in all his glory. She would give him Nikos's face, with his chiseled cheekbones and proud nose, his square jaw and sensual mouth. Even his ears were attractive. Her fingers itched to begin.

"What are you thinking, I wonder, as you stare at me so intently?"

The words jerked Lexi out of her reverie and she realized she *had* been staring at him. He bit into a juicy strawberry as he considered her, and she found herself transfixed by the sight. How would he taste if she were to kiss him right now? Like sweet berries, or something darker and more potent?

"I'm sorry," she said, sounding a little breathless. She cleared her throat and strove for a breezy, offhand tone. "I was just thinking how handsome you are. In fact, I think you're the most attractive man I've ever seen." Oh, God. Did that really come out of her mouth? She'd obviously spent too much time in her studio, away from people. She laughed, embarrassed by her own gushing. "I'm sure you've heard that a million times, right?"

He gave a philosophical shrug and sliced a thin wedge of cheese, neither confirming nor denying her words. "It's always interesting to me what people find attractive. Maybe when you get to know me better, you won't think I'm quite so handsome."

Lexi sincerely doubted that. She didn't know what she found most appealing about him—his physical appearance or the sound of his voice. She felt herself vibrating when he spoke. His English was perfect, but she loved his sexy accent and decided she could happily listen to him talk all day. The thought of getting to know this guy on any level caused a tornado of butterflies to unfurl in her stomach.

Just the fact that she was having lunch with him made her want to pinch herself to be sure she wasn't dreaming.

"I doubt that would ever happen," she said. She paused, her glass halfway to her mouth. "Wait. Are you suggesting that we'll have the opportunity to get to know each other?"

He smiled, revealing a deep dimple in one cheek. Something shifted in Lexi's chest at the sight.

"I'm going to be spending a lot of time working here—it only makes sense that we'll get to know each other," he said. "If you'd like to, that is."

Lexi felt as if she stood on the edge of a precipice, and one unwary step would send her plummeting over the edge. Her heart began to thump hard at the implicit suggestion in his voice. Did she want to get to know Nikos Christakos on a personal level? On an intimate level, unless she was misreading the expression in his eyes? She wasn't sure. He was too gorgeous, too intimidating. He made her pulse race and her mouth go dry just looking at him. Beyond that, there was a certain comfort in not knowing too much about him. She could imagine him however she wanted, without the fear of his human imperfections—if he had any—ruining her perception of him. Right now, at this moment, he was the ideal man.

But to pass up such an opportunity…she would never again meet anyone like him in her life, she was sure. She could limit their relationship to a platonic lunch on this patio, but she would always wonder what else she might have missed. She'd never had a relationship based solely on physical attraction, but now she wondered if it might not have its benefits. She didn't know if she was the kind of woman who could separate her emotions from sex, but she knew she would regret it if she just walked away.

Besides, Nelda had been right about one thing—getting

to know Nikos would mean she would have easy access to him for her sculpture, even if he refused to sit for her.

Drawing a deep breath, she stepped out over the edge. "Yes," she said, letting her eyes search his. "I would like to get to know you better. A lot better, actually."

AN HOUR LATER, NIKOS CARRIED the picnic basket back into the house. While he had eaten two of the Caprese sandwiches and nearly all the fruit, Lexi had found her stomach in a sudden tangle of nerves. She had picked at the fruit and hadn't done justice to either the sandwich or the dessert. If Nikos had noticed, he didn't comment. He'd kept up a comfortable stream of conversation, talking first about the weather and then about the work he was doing on the house. Lexi had latched on to the subject gratefully, and now she followed him inside and looked around at the empty rooms. The interior was similar in layout and style to her own house, except that the previous owners had painted everything in pastel colors and had installed wall-to-wall carpeting throughout.

"So what are you going to do in here?" she asked, indicating the main living room with its wide double doors and abundance of painted woodwork.

Nikos came to stand beside her, so close that she could smell the sunscreen he had applied earlier, warm and fragrant now from the heat of his skin. She breathed deeply, hoping he didn't notice.

"First, I'm going to strip away this paint to reveal the natural wood," he said, gesturing expansively with his hands. "There are beautiful hardwood floors beneath this carpeting, so I'll expose them, as well."

"I thought it was strange that everything has been painted," she mused. "My own house still has the original finish on the woodwork."

"You're fortunate," Nikos said. "How long have you lived there?"

Lexi grimaced. "Almost thirty years. I grew up in that house. My parents passed away several years ago and left the property to me." She sensed his surprise. "Trust me," she said drily, "I could never afford to live there otherwise. I'm sure that if I had brothers and sisters, the house would have been sold after my parents died. But, it's just me, and I love the house and the neighborhood. I've had offers from real estate agents, but I've never wanted to sell."

Even with the floundering economy, Santa Barbara had retained its home values, and the houses on the street where Lexi lived were some of the most desirable, situated on what was referred to as the American Riviera. The house that Nikos was restoring had been listed for over a million dollars, which meant that whoever had hired him to do the restoration work could afford to pay him well. No wonder he hadn't been interested in modeling for her; he probably had no need for the extra money.

"I'd like to see the inside of your house," he remarked.

Lexi knew he didn't mean right then, but suddenly she was reluctant to have the afternoon end. "Well, if you have time, I could show it to you now. I mean, if you don't have to get back to work right away."

He grinned, his teeth white against his tanned skin. "I set my own hours. Besides, I can always call it job-related research."

Lexi was acutely conscious of him as he followed her outside and along the sidewalk to her own home. But when she glanced back at him, she saw his eyes were on her house, and not on her.

"Was this built by the Green brothers?" he asked, standing back to survey her home with appreciative eyes.

"I don't know," Lexi confessed. "It's been in my family for ages."

The two-story bungalow was small by any standards, but what it lacked in size, it made up for in charm and character. They climbed the front steps until they stood on the wide, covered veranda, and Nikos took a moment to admire the substantial columns that supported the overhanging roof.

"The craftsmanship is amazing," he commented, indicating the ceiling of the veranda. He leaned over the low wall to peer up at the side of the house. "Look at the decorative knee braces and elaborated rafter ends. Very nice."

Lexi raised an eyebrow, amused in spite of herself. Had she really thought he might be interested in her? With a soft huff of laughter, she pushed open the front door and stepped inside. He followed her, and although he didn't immediately say anything, she could sense his delight with the house. The floor plan was spacious, and the living room flowed into the dining room and kitchen, with lots of windows and doors to the exterior veranda and back deck.

Lexi's own decorating style ran to the simplistic, partly because she couldn't be bothered to maintain a fussy home, and mostly because she didn't want anything to detract from the natural beauty of the interior. A large stone fireplace dominated the living room with built-in cabinetry and bookcases on either side. Beamed ceilings gave the rooms a cozy, rustic look. Through the wide doors that led to the dining room, there were more built-ins, including a china cabinet and buffet, and a simple wainscot with a plate rail.

Taking the basket from him, she set it down on the dining table and watched as Nikos walked through the rooms. He looked at everything, sometimes running his fingertips along a cabinet or molding. His touch was almost reverent, and Lexi knew a moment of intense envy that her woodwork should elicit such awe. What would it be like to have him touch her with such deference?

"Would you like to see the upstairs?" she asked carefully. "There are just two bedrooms and a bathroom, but they've been maintained in near-original condition. Except for the bathroom. The original claw-foot tub is still there, but I had a shower installed several years ago for practical reasons."

He turned to her then, and his green eyes drifted over her in a way that told Lexi he was imagining her in that tub. "You don't like taking baths?"

"Oh, no," she protested. "I love soaking in a tub, but not when it's eight o'clock in the morning and I'm already late for work. I save that luxury for the evening, when I need to relax."

"Hmm." The sound was like a hum of approval deep in his throat. "I'd like to see that. Your upstairs, I mean."

Lexi knew exactly what he meant.

"This way." She led him up the twisting staircase, her heart starting to thud unevenly in her chest. When she risked a glance over her shoulder at him, she saw his eyes were on her and not on the carved banister or handcrafted newel posts. He reminded her of a large, predatory cat. Even when she caught him staring, he didn't look away.

Lexi shivered. Logic told her that she didn't know the first thing about this guy. She should have her head examined for inviting a virtual stranger into her home. But instinct told her that she didn't need to be afraid of Nikos. He wouldn't do anything she wasn't completely ready for. But the expression in his eyes as he watched her caused her heart to thump unsteadily and a slow heat to slide beneath her skin.

"Here we are," she said as they reached the top of the

staircase. Her voice sounded breathless. Nikos came to stand beside her, dwarfing the upper landing with his height and sheer presence. "The bathroom is at the end of the hall."

But instead of walking to the door that Lexi indicated, he entered the nearest room. "Is this where you sleep?"

"Yes." Lexi stepped into the room behind Nikos, seeing it through his eyes. She'd purchased the massive iron sleigh bed after she'd sold her first sculpture. It dominated the room, flanked by deep windows and heaped with pillows and a lofty down comforter. An upholstered chair occupied one corner of the room, and Lexi had grouped a half dozen pillar candles and votives on a small table under a far window, with the breathtaking views of Santa Barbara and the sea in the distance. Sunlight dappled the hardwood floors and cast bright blocks of light across the bed.

"You're a romantic," Nikos said, glancing around the room.

"Oh, no," Lexi protested with a small laugh. "I am definitely a realist."

"You say that with such certainty."

He turned to look at her with a new intensity in his expression, as if she somehow puzzled him. Lexi tucked a strand of hair behind one ear, feeling inexplicably shy. Here she was, in her bedroom, with possibly the world's most gorgeous man staring at her with a mixture of amusement and lazy interest.

"Yes, well, I guess I've heard it enough times that I actually believe it," she said, laughing self-consciously.

She was unprepared when he put a finger beneath her chin and tipped her face up. His expression was so intense that Lexi stopped breathing. He searched her face for a moment, his eyes drifting over her features and lingering on her mouth.

"Well, I don't believe it," he murmured softly.

"You don't?" Lexi heard herself ask. Her voice sounded breathy and low, almost hypnotized. "Why not?"

"Because a realist wouldn't wear such a sexy red dress, or put together such a delicious picnic lunch, or look at me the way you're looking at me right now."

Lexi felt her insides begin to liquefy. "How am I looking at you?" she whispered, but if her body's helpless response to him was any indication, she already knew.

Nikos took a step closer, until she could feel his heat and see the individual gold-and-brown stubble just visible on his jaw. With his finger still beneath her chin, he slid his free hand through her hair to cup the nape of her neck.

"Like you want me to kiss you," he murmured softly, and bending his head, he covered her mouth with his own.

The touch of his lips completed her internal meltdown, and with a soft sigh, Lexi leaned into him. She didn't know what she had been expecting, but nothing could have prepared her for the potency of his kiss. With one hand still cradling her head, his other hand slid to her back and drew her closer. Completely surrounded by his heat, hardness and scent, Lexi could only cling mindlessly to him. His mouth was warm and firm, moving with seductive gentleness over hers, urging her lips apart to allow for the intrusion of his tongue.

Lexi heard herself make a low, moaning sound of pleasure, and her hands curled around his arms, her fingers digging into his hard triceps. He deepened the kiss, his tongue sliding hotly against hers while his fingers buried themselves in her hair and angled her head for better access. Lexi wanted to consume him, to wind her body around his and give herself over to the incredible sensations he aroused in her. Her blood pulsed thickly in her veins and heat bloomed low in her abdomen as he explored her mouth.

When Nikos finally lifted his head, she felt dazed and a little unsteady. He didn't release her, but stroked his thumb along her jaw. His eyes looked sleepy with desire and when he spoke, his voice was a husky rasp.

"Just how well would you like us to get to know each other?" One corner of his delectable mouth lifted in a half smile, but Lexi sensed the tightly coiled tension in his body as he waited for her answer.

The heat in his expression, combined with the touch of his fingers along her cheek, made it difficult for her to recall why getting involved with Nikos was a bad idea. He was too gorgeous to resist. Did she have the ability to keep her emotions under tight wraps and not fall for this guy? She didn't know; she only knew that she wanted him more than she could recall ever wanting another man. Even Ethan hadn't made her feel this sweet, insistent urgency. She had no doubt that once she got to know the real Nikos, she would be disappointed by what she found, but right now she didn't care.

"Let's just say that since I saw you that first day, I've been dying to get my hands on you," she finally said, daring to meet his eyes and emboldened by what she saw there. "I want to know every inch of you."

"That sounds perfect," he said simply, and bent his head to hers.

4

HER LIPS WERE INCREDIBLY SOFT and she tasted like a combination of sweet strawberries and lemon. Nikos really did feel like the Big Bad Wolf, his desire to devour her was so strong. Even the knowledge that he was behaving like a complete hypocrite couldn't diminish the lust that swamped him.

He wasn't unaware of his own looks, or the fact that others found him attractive, but he'd made a promise to himself eight years ago not to use his looks to take advantage of others, or to let others exploit him. But right now, with Lexi Adams making soft moans of pleasure as he kissed her, he didn't care what her reasons were for wanting him. He couldn't remember the last time he'd had such an urgent need to see a woman spread out beneath him, and he desperately wanted to see if Lexi came close to the fantasy images he had of her in his head.

He buried his fingers in her silky hair, angling his mouth across hers for deeper penetration. She made a noise of approval and stroked her tongue against his, sliding one hand to the nape of his neck. Her fingers were cool against his heated skin. Nikos dragged his mouth from hers and sucked in a steadying breath. He needed to slow down, because as much as he wanted Lexi, he also wanted to savor every moment of what was to come.

"I want to see you," she whispered on a ragged exhale. "I want to see all of you."

Her dark eyes were a little hazy with pleasure, and her mouth was moist from his kisses. Nikos immediately reached a hand behind his head and grabbed a fistful of his T-shirt, dragging it off. Lexi helped him, pushing it up over his chest and then letting her hands linger on his skin.

"You are so beautiful," she breathed, her gaze raking over his body. She traced a fingertip down the deep groove that bisected his torso, admiring his pecs and stomach. "I could just look at you forever."

In all the years that Nikos had deliberately used his body to make a living, he'd rarely felt an emotional connection with any of the women who had admired him or tried to get closer to him. In fact, he'd felt a certain amount of disdain for them, especially toward the end, when he'd finally matured enough to realize they didn't really care about *him*. But with Lexi, it didn't seem to matter if she was only interested in his body; he wanted to give her whatever she desired. He didn't know the first thing about her, but everything about her appealed to him. He wanted her more than he'd wanted any woman in a very long time.

"You can do more than just look." He smiled, using the back of his knuckles to sweep her hair from her face. Her expression was one of feminine desire, and Nikos felt his body harden in response. "Tell me what you want."

"I want you to kiss me again," she entreated softly, and reached up to wind her arms around his neck.

Nikos gave a groan of surrender and, bending his head, fused his lips to hers. At the same time, he lifted her into his arms. She made a startled sound of surprise and clutched at his shoulders as he made his way across the room to her bed. She laughed as he lowered a knee onto the mattress and laid her across the comforter, and then collapsed beside her, pretending to have strained himself with the effort.

"I'm just kidding," he reassured her with a grin, rolling toward her. "You don't weigh that much."

"Come here," she said, laughing.

She welcomed him into her arms as naturally as if they'd been lovers for years, although he would have staked his life on the fact that making love with a virtual stranger wasn't something Lexi Adams made a habit of. Even now, as he studied her face, she swept her lashes down, hiding her eyes from him. He pressed his mouth against each fragile eyelid, hearing her uneven breathing and knowing that if he slid his hand over her breast, he would feel the frantic beat of her heart against his palm. Instead, he dragged his mouth along the curve of her cheek and then teased her lips with his tongue, licking and kissing their plumpness. With a soft gasp, she turned her head to follow the trail he made, seeking more of the sensual contact. Nikos complied, slanting his mouth across hers and kissing her deeply. She arched against him and her hands slid over his shoulders, her fingers smoothing down his back.

Rolling to his side, Nikos pulled Lexi with him, one hand sliding along her hip until his fingers encountered the smooth, cool skin of her thigh. Capturing her leg, he draped it across his hips as he continued to kiss her. She moaned and pushed closer, clutching at his back. Lust, hot and urgent, jackknifed through his gut. His cock throbbed where he pressed against her center and all he could think about was driving himself into her heat. She'd be tight and slick, and he wanted to see her lose control.

Nikos raised his head and stared down at her. Afternoon sunlight slanted through the nearby window and bathed her skin in a warm glow. Her irises were almost black, with tiny copper splotches near the pupil, like gold coins tossed into a deep well. Right now, her eyes were cloudy with pleasure, and her pale skin had taken on a faint flush of color. Her breathing came in soft pants against his neck, and her fingertips smoothed distracted circles over his shoulder blades.

She shifted closer, hitching her leg higher over his hip. Nikos couldn't resist sliding his hand along the silken length of her thigh until he encountered the edge of her panties. He wanted to slip his fingers beneath the elastic and stroke the soft skin of her buttocks. He wanted to push the fragile fabric aside and explore her cleft. Was she already damp with need? He ached to find out. Instead, he cupped her rear in his hand and kneaded the firm flesh through the satin fabric until she moaned into his mouth and pressed even closer. Despite her delicate appearance, she gripped him with surprising strength.

Breaking the kiss, she pulled back enough to look at him. "I want to see you," she breathed.

Before Nikos could guess her intent, she pushed him onto his back and rose above him, hiking her dress over her legs as she straddled his thighs. He lay back against the pillows, watching her as she devoured him with her eyes.

"Oh, man," she said softly, smoothing her palms over his abdomen and chest. "You're incredible. Your skin is like hot silk, but underneath you're so hard."

She had no idea.

All she had to do was glance down to see the evidence of his raging arousal. She was caressing his body, both with her hands and her eyes, tracing her fingers over his ribs and chest, and lingering on the sensitive nubs of his nipples. Her eyes reflected feminine desire, and he felt himself harden even more beneath her appreciative gaze.

How long was it since he'd been this jacked for a woman? He'd made a mistake in coming home with her, he knew that. Everything in him screamed that she was no different than any of the other women who had wanted him solely for his looks and for the sexual pleasure he could give them. But he'd been helpless to refuse her offer. For the first time in years, he'd found himself fantasizing about a woman and anticipating what it would be like to fit his body to hers, to give her pleasure and absorb her soft cries as she came apart in his arms. He wasn't with her for the sole purpose of assuaging his own physical needs; instead, he wanted to fulfill every one of hers.

Growing up on the island of Syros, Nikos had known there was something unique about his appearance, but when he'd looked in the mirror, he'd seen nothing extraordinary. At fourteen, he'd been tall for his age. Working with his father and uncles as part of their construction crew had strengthened and defined his muscles so that he could have easily passed for someone several years older. But nobody could have been more shocked than him when he was approached by a middle-aged Englishwoman who said she wanted to make Nikos an international sensation.

He had been helping his father do repairs on one of the island's resort hotels, and had noticed one of the guests watching him over the course of several days, even going so far as to take his photo. But when his father had confronted the woman, she had introduced herself as a top modeling agent and had provided both Nikos and his father with her card and credentials. Georgina Caldwell had offered Nikos a lucrative contract if he would accompany her to London. He had flatly refused, but his father had been interested in hearing more, especially about the income. He'd swept all Nikos's protests aside, insisting this opportunity would provide his son with a better life than he could give him.

Within a week, against his will, Nikos had found himself on a flight to England. He never saw the island of Syros again. He'd lived in a tiny apartment with seven other male models, and his days were filled with casting calls or fittings, posing for photo shoots or walking the runway. At night, there were parties and shows, and almost in spite of himself, Nikos became caught up in the glamorous lifestyle.

When he was fifteen, he'd lost his virginity to a woman nearly twice his age. By the time he was seventeen, his face had graced the cover of dozens of magazines and he'd landed several lucrative advertising campaigns. By the time he turned twenty, he'd appeared in numerous television commercials and had been the face of a leading men's fragrance, a top clothing designer and a luxury-car manufacturer. He was earning close to a million dollars a year by his twenty-fourth birthday, when he'd abruptly decided that he'd had enough. Sex had become routine and meaningless, recreational drugs and alcohol the norm, and it had taken the senseless death of a friend and fellow model to make him realize he was wasting his life.

He'd quit modeling that very day, despite the fact he'd had to pay an exorbitant sum of money to the agency for breach of contract. Looking back, it had been worth every penny.

He'd come to Santa Barbara because that was where several of his cousins had settled years earlier, but soon found the climate was similar to that of Syros. His cousins operated a small construction business, doing restoration work on older homes. Nikos had joined them and had enjoyed the physical demands of the job. But it hadn't been long before he realized they weren't being faithful to the original plans of the historic homes, and the knowledge had frustrated him. So he'd taken a couple of courses at a local architectural school. Soon, he was enrolled full-time. He'd learned the history of the various building styles and, more important, how to restore the old houses to their original condition. Eventually, he'd started his own business and his cousins had come to work for him. That had been eight years ago, and while he missed the island of Syros, he knew he would never return. He'd left his innocence there, and going back seemed like a sacrilege.

Watching Lexi, he realized she was the first woman he'd truly desired in years. He loved sex, but having gorged himself on beautiful women during his modeling years, like a greedy child at a dessert banquet, he'd come away feeling malnourished and a little ill. During the last eight years, he'd been selective about who he slept with, but sex had never been anything more than a pleasurable physical release.

Lexi, on the other hand, intrigued him. Even her request for him to model for her couldn't dampen his body's response. He wanted to know her better and, contrary to how he felt about modeling, he wanted her to see him—all of him. He wanted her to find him as sexy and irresistible as he found her.

Now Lexi's fingers traced the contours of his abdominal muscles until they reached the waistband of his jeans and lingered there. Her eyes were on the unmistakable bulge behind his zipper. Her lips parted and slowly, as if afraid he might try to stop her, she laid her hand over him. Nikos groaned and barely restrained himself from arching into her palm.

Her eyes flew to his face. "May I?"

Nikos held his breath as Lexi unfastened the button on his jeans and slowly drew the zipper down. But when she spread the denim aside and cupped him through the thin fabric of his boxers, he nearly came off the mattress. He wanted to turn her beneath him on the bed, drag her panties off and bury himself in her heat. Instead, he linked his arms behind his head and let her do as she pleased, although it was more difficult to control his ragged breathing and hammering pulse.

"I want to undress you," Lexi said, and scrambled off the bed to unlace his boots, dragging his socks off with them. Then she climbed back over him on all fours, until her hands were braced on either side of his head and her dark hair hung around their faces like a curtain. She fixed her gaze on his mouth before slowly lowering her head and covering his lips with her own.

Nikos had intended to let her take the lead and set the pace, but her kiss was like a drug, sucking his willpower out of him and making rational thought almost impossible. With a deep groan of surrender, he caught her face in his hands, thrusting his fingers into the cool, silky mass of her hair and deepening the kiss. Lexi lowered herself onto him, until her breasts pressed his chest and the ridge of his erection strained against her center.

"You feel so good," he muttered against her mouth. When she slid experimentally along the length of his rigid cock, he gave a hiss of pleasure and reached down to grip her hips and guide her movements.

"Omigod," Lexi breathed, and settled herself more fully against him.

Nikos slid his hands beneath her skirt and cupped her rear, stroking and squeezing her pliant flesh. She gasped into his mouth and her movements became more urgent. Reaching between her shoulder blades, Nikos found the zipper at the back of her dress and drew it down until the fabric gaped away from her body and he could see her pink-tipped breasts.

Nikos broke the kiss and pushed her to a sitting position. Hooking his fingers in the straps of her dress, he pulled them downward. The bodice caught briefly on her nipples, and then fell in a soft whisper of fabric around her waist. Nikos let his breath out, and covered her breasts with his hands, testing their weight and gently kneading them. They were just large enough to fill his palms, and he rubbed his thumbs across the distended tips, hearing her soft hiss of pleasure.

"Take this off," he commanded softly.

Lexi complied, pulling the dress over her head before she tossed it onto the floor. Just as he'd imagined, she was slender and pale, her skin flawless. She looked down at him through hazy eyes, and caught his hands in hers, drawing them back up to cover her breasts.

"Touch me," she breathed. "I want to feel your hands on me."

With a soft growl, Nikos sat up and wrapped his arms around her as he crushed his mouth to hers, sliding his tongue along hers and feasting on her lips until he thought he'd burst with need. Her skin was warm and silken against his, and he skated his fingers over her back, exploring the dips and curves of her body, gratified when she shifted restlessly and tried to get even closer.

"Here, let's try this," he said, and turned her onto her back. He knelt between her splayed thighs and drank in the sight of her against the pillows. With her black hair spread out around her and her dark eyes shimmering with need, she exceeded his lustful imaginings. When her gaze dropped meaningfully to his jeans, he didn't pretend to misunderstand, pushing them down and off, until he was able to drop them onto the floor beside her dress.

She gave a soft "oh" of admiration, and reached out to slide her fingers beneath the waistband of his boxers and tug them down, releasing his erection. Nikos gritted his teeth as she stroked the head of his penis and then closed her hand around him, squeezing him gently. He sucked air into his lungs and struggled for control, but the sight of her slim, pale fingers around the flushed length of his cock was too erotic. With a soft growl, he wrapped a hand around her wrist and pulled her away, using his free hand to shove his boxers down over his thighs. He rose above her, bracing his weight on one arm as he kicked his underwear completely free. Naked, he settled himself into the cradle of her hips. She stared at him with a mixture of desire and anticipation that he found impossible to resist.

"Are you sure about this?" he asked softly, tracing his thumb over the plumpness of her lower lip. "No regrets later?"

Turning her face, she caught the pad of his thumb between her teeth and bit gently, before drawing the digit into her mouth and sucking on it. The sensation caused a white-hot bolt of lust to ricochet through his body and settle in his groin, where he pulsed hotly. Whatever illusions he'd had of letting her set the pace were obliterated with each soft, hot sweep of her tongue.

"I'm sure," she assured him, releasing his thumb and reaching for him. "Whatever happens later, I won't regret this."

5

NIKOS GRUNTED HIS APPROVAL AND replaced his thumb with his mouth, kissing her so deeply that their teeth scraped together as he stroked her tongue with his own. At the same time, he slid a hand to her rear, cupping her and lifting her against his hardness. Lexi didn't know what she'd been expecting, but Nikos completely consumed her until she could no longer think straight.

"I want you inside me," she breathed against his mouth, and reached between their bodies to curl her fingers around his thick length. He made a constricted sound of pleasure and Lexi felt her own desire kick into full gear as she stroked him. The thick veins in his shaft pulsed beneath her fingers, and when she ran the tip of one finger over the engorged head, it came away slick with moisture.

"Enough," he rasped into her ear, "or I won't last."

Nikos dragged his mouth away from hers and lowered his head to her shoulder. Lexi felt him shudder lightly before he rolled to his side, pulling Lexi with him.

"Take these off," he commanded hoarsely, and pushed her underwear down over her hips.

Lexi helped him, until she was able to kick the garment free, and then she was as nude as Nikos.

"You're exactly as I'd imagined," he said huskily, and splayed his hand over her abdomen, just above the narrow strip of curls.

His palm was warm and callused against her skin, and when he slid his hand lower, she spread her thighs so that he could cup her intimately. She ached with need, and pushed against his hand to tell him without words that she wanted more. But when he parted her folds and slid a finger over her slick flesh, she gasped from the shock of pleasure that jolted through her.

"You are so wet," he rasped.

He swirled a finger over her clitoris, causing her hips to jerk, but when he inserted a finger inside her she nearly came off the mattress.

"Oh," she breathed, "yes! That feels so good."

Nikos gave a groan and covered her mouth with his as he pumped his finger slowly into her. Lexi kissed him greedily, drawing on his tongue and spearing her fingers through his hair. Tension coiled tightly inside her with each sensual stroke.

"I'm not going to last," she managed to gasp. "I want you inside me when I come."

He muttered something in Greek that sounded like a curse. "I have no protection," he grated, clearly frustrated.

"Bedside drawer," Lexi told him. She'd kept a supply of condoms for the nights when Ethan had stayed over, but that had been more than six months ago. She had no idea if prophylactics had a shelf life, but there was no way she was going to mention it to Nikos and give him an excuse to end the encounter.

Leaning across her, he jerked the small drawer open and fished around until he withdrew a box of condoms. He gave her a single questioning look before he dumped the box upside down and took one of the small packets and tore it open with his teeth.

Lexi watched as he covered himself, the sight of his strong hands on his erection incredibly arousing. He shifted so that he was directly above her. Bracing his weight on one arm, he positioned himself at her entrance. His features were taut, and his light green eyes seemed to glow in his face. His entire body was primed and ready, every muscle standing out in stark definition. Aroused, Nikos Christakos took her breath away.

He fitted the wide, warm head of his penis at her opening, and with his gaze locked on her, he slowly surged forward. Lexi sucked in her breath. The thick, hot slide of him inside her caused her to arch instinctively upward.

"You're so tight," he muttered, his accent more pronounced. Hooking a hand beneath her thigh, he drew her leg up and over his hip as he began to move. He stretched her, filled her, eased himself into her until her buttocks were flush against his hips and there was nothing but the taste, scent and feel of Nikos in her and surrounding her.

"You're beautiful," he breathed against her lips. "Are you okay?"

In answer, Lexi arched against him and drew both legs up until her heels rested on his firm, taut butt. The movement opened her even more, and when she shifted her hips restlessly beneath him, he groaned and buried his face in her neck. "I'm more than okay," she assured him, and he plunged into her. The sensation of him filling her was more exquisitely intense than anything she had ever experienced.

"Kiss me." He turned his face and caught her lips in a kiss that nearly undid her. He drew on her tongue even as his pace quickened and he thrust into her with increasing urgency.

Lexi heard a desperate mewling sound and realized

with a sense of shock that it came from her. Nikos pushed one of her legs to the side, and then reached between their bodies to slide a finger over her slick center. Sensation, pure and raw, spiraled through her, causing her to cry out and writhe beneath him.

"Come," he growled, and punctuated the word with another bone-melting surge of his hips against hers.

Shock waves of erotic pleasure coursed through her as he thrust harder, faster, and she could feel a climax beginning to throb in her clitoris. But when he stroked his finger over her, it was her undoing. With a choked sob, she convulsed around him as her orgasm tore through her in a blinding rush of pleasure.

The intensity of her release was enough to push Nikos over the edge as well, and with a hoarse shout, he plunged into her and then stiffened, and his body shuddered above hers. He dropped his head to her shoulder, and Lexi hugged him against her. Their breathing was ragged and she could feel the heavy, uneven thumping of his heart against her chest. He pressed a kiss against her neck, just at the juncture of her jaw. His breath, warm and fresh, washed over her as he dragged air into his lungs.

"That was...amazing." Carefully, he withdrew from her and discarded the condom before rolling to his side, pulling her with him and tucking her back against his chest. He dipped his head and caught her earlobe between his teeth, nipping gently, then soothing the tender flesh with his lips and tongue.

Amazing didn't come close to describing what Lexi had just experienced. Simply put, the sex had been the hottest, most incredible she'd ever had. Even Ethan, as skilled as he had been, had never aroused her as much as this man. Delicious aftershocks still trembled through her body, and her heart thudded hard in her chest. But as good as the sex had been, she had no illusion it was anything more than that. She didn't know Nikos at all, and there was no reason to expect that she would have any kind of relationship with him. Even if she wanted to, her work would consume most of her time.

"I have a suggestion," Nikos murmured in her ear as he stroked his fingers over her arm.

Lexi twisted her face until she could see him. He had propped his head on one hand and looked down at her with a warm expression on his handsome face. "What is it?"

"It's almost four o'clock. I think we should try out that claw-foot tub in the bathroom."

Lexi's eyes widened, and she laughed uncertainly. "I'm not sure… You're so large."

Nikos pressed a kiss against her mouth. "I think we can manage, and then afterward, if you're hungry, I'll cook you something to eat."

Lexi ignored the way her heart leaped, determined to keep her emotions in check. It would be easy to fall for a guy like Nikos, but she reminded herself that she knew next to nothing about him. She wouldn't let herself get too attached to him. But right now, the lure of soaping his magnificent body with her bare hands outweighed any other concerns she had.

"Mmm," she murmured against his lips. "How can I refuse an offer like that?"

TUCKING THE PILLOW BENEATH HER cheek, Lexi watched as Nikos pulled his jeans on. His hair was still wet from his recent shower, and she could see droplets of moisture on his shoulders. It was barely 5:00 a.m. and still dark outside. Nikos had stayed the entire night. They'd taken a bath, as he'd suggested, which had led to another erotic interlude. Afterward, he had commandeered her kitchen and rummaged through her cupboards and refrigerator until he'd found enough ingredients to make a delicious stir-fry. He had pulled the meal together effortlessly, and Lexi could see that he was completely comfortable in the kitchen.

They'd spent the evening entwined on the sofa, sipping wine and talking, and watching the sun sink over the Pacific through the wide windows. Nikos had seemed preoccupied with touching her. The contact was always light and nonthreatening; he played with her fingers, or traced the outline of her ear, or wound her hair around his fingertip, but he maintained an almost constant physical contact with her. Lexi had decided it must be a European thing, and she'd found it disconcerting at first. But when he'd stopped, she missed it. The hours had slipped by, and when she'd smothered a yawn, he had stood to leave. Knowing she'd be exhausted and irritable in the morning, but not caring, she had asked him to stay.

She'd forgotten how wonderful it felt to have a warm, hard body next to hers during the night, and how magical the darkness became when masculine hands reached for her. Like velvet, the shadows had swallowed her soft cries and his husky words of approval.

Now she watched as he dressed, admiring the play of muted light across his muscles. His body was imprinted on her skin, and if she closed her eyes she could still feel the slope of his spine and the firm thrust of his buttocks beneath her palms. Straightening, he caught her watching him and came over to sit on the edge of the mattress.

"I didn't mean to wake you," he said, reaching out to stroke the hair back from her face. "I think it's better if I leave now, before the neighborhood wakes up and sees me."

Lexi smiled. Right now, she couldn't bring herself to

care what the neighbors thought. "Are you working next door today?"

Nikos nodded and laced his fingers with hers. "My cousins will arrive in a few hours. What about you?"

"I'll be at my studio, working on my latest sculpture. You've inspired me."

He went silent and stared moodily at their entwined fingers. After a moment, he withdrew his hand and gave her a brief smile. "Well, I'm glad to be of service."

He stood up, and Lexi had a moment of panic that somehow, this was the end. She wouldn't see him again. Reaching out, she caught him by the wrist.

"Hey, did I say something wrong?" she asked. "I only meant that you've energized me—gotten my creative juices flowing." She slanted him an amused look. "So to speak."

He responded by carrying her hand to his mouth and turning it over to press a warm kiss against the palm. "Thank you for last night."

"Will I see you again?" She hoped her voice didn't sound as anxious as she felt.

"You can see me anytime you want," he replied. "I'll be right next door."

6

Lexi drove to her studio while it was still dark, consumed by thoughts of Nikos. Inside the cavernous space, she quickly punched the security code into the keypad next to the door, then flipped on the lights and raised the shades on the enormous windows. Pulling the dust cloth away from the half-finished sculpture, she circled it slowly, surveying it through critical eyes. She traced her fingers along the crosshatch marks made by her chisel. She'd roughed out the figure, but now she was ready to begin refining the piece, and with Nikos's face and form still fresh in her mind, she knew exactly where to begin. She was glad that she'd selected a slab with large crystals, which would impart a brilliant finish to the completed work.

Slowly, as the first rays of sunlight began to lighten the studio, she arranged her tools on a rolling table nearby. She began chiseling the stone with care and precision, stopping every so often to step back and scrutinize her progress. She might not have Nikos here to model for her, but she had her vivid memories of the previous night and they were more than adequate. As her hands worked the stone, she could almost feel his firm muscles beneath her fingers. If she faltered, or became uncertain about a particular chisel stroke, she had only to close her eyes to imagine him, and her hands became sure again.

She worked steadily until her stomach finally prompted her to take a break and go in search of something to eat. Glancing at her watch, she was shocked to see it was nearly five o'clock in the afternoon. She'd been at it for more than ten hours, and although she'd become engrossed in her sculptures before, she rarely forgot to eat. Setting her tools aside, she went to the kitchenette that had been installed in one corner of the warehouse studio. Rummaging through the cupboards and the small refrigerator, she found a packet of crackers and a block of cheese, and fixed herself a quick snack. As she ate, she considered the sculpture.

Typically, when she created her classical-Greek gods, she started at the top and worked her way toward the base, and this piece was no different. To her, the face was the most critical part of the sculpture and she couldn't really visualize the physique until she had the facial features in place.

She realized now that the reason she'd struggled with this particular work was because she hadn't been able to visualize the face. But then she'd met Nikos and everything had become clear. Already, the bone structure was taking shape beneath her chisel, and she knew she'd made the right choice. Her hands had flown over the marble, chipping a bit here and there, defining the brow or the thrust of a cheekbone. Nikos's face was beginning to emerge from the stone. At the rate she was going, she'd be ready to start on the body in just a few days.

She still had several hours of good light remaining, but she suddenly found herself eager to get home. She didn't know what time Nikos stopped working, and she wanted to see him before he left.

Covering the sculpture with the dust cloth, she lowered the shades and flipped off the lights. Her studio was located in a row of warehouses on the outskirts of Santa Barbara, and the drive home would take thirty minutes. As she pulled into her driveway, she saw Nikos's truck parked on the curb next door. Climbing out of the car, she debated going into the house to take a quick shower, since she was covered in a fine layer of dust. But afraid she might miss him, she drew a deep breath and walked along the sidewalk to the front porch. She could hear the sound of a hammer from inside the house, and she carefully pushed the door open and stepped into the hallway. Nikos knelt on the hardwood floor in the living room, carefully replacing several boards from a stack beside him. Gone was the wall-to-wall carpeting, and just as he had promised, he had exposed the gleaming mahogany beneath.

"Wow," she breathed. "What a transformation."

Nikos rocked back on his heels, his expression registering surprise. "Lexi."

"I'm sorry. I heard you hammering and let myself in." Suddenly appalled at her own pushiness, she grimaced. "I hope you don't mind."

"No, of course not." He set the hammer aside and rose to his feet in one fluid movement, swiping his hands on his thighs. "I've been waiting for you. I mean, I was going to come over and see you when you got home."

Lexi reached out and put a steadying hand on the door frame. Would she always feel this light-headed whenever she saw him? "Really? I was afraid I would miss you. Not that I didn't miss you—I did. But obviously you're here, so I didn't miss you—" She broke abruptly off, aware that she was babbling. "Forget it. I was afraid that you might have already left."

Stepping toward her, he reached out and wiped his

thumb over her cheek, smiling down at her. "You have chalk on your face."

Lexi stared at him. He hadn't shaved, and the shadow of beard on his jaw gave him a faintly piratical look that she found wildly attractive. In contrast to his sun-streaked hair, his eyebrows and lashes were dark, making his light green eyes all the more startling. She wanted to press her mouth to the indent in his cheek.

She raised a self-conscious hand to her face. "I just came from my studio," she explained, laughing a little. "I should probably go home and clean up."

"Don't." Grasping her by the shoulders, he made a show of inspecting her. "You look perfect." His smile widened. "You're covered in white powder."

"It's marble dust."

Nikos took her hands in his and turned them palm up. He stroked his thumbs across the roughened pads of her fingers.

Embarrassed, Lexi pulled her hands free and curled them at her sides. "Sorry."

"Don't be. I like the way they feel on my skin."

Immediately, heat swamped her as images of the previous night flooded her memory. She had loved touching him. In fact, she had spent most of the night exploring his amazing body with her hands and mouth. Neither of them had gotten much sleep, and yet she'd woken up feeling energized and eager to get to work. As she looked at him now, warmth bloomed beneath her skin and flowed through her limbs like liquid honey. She wanted him. That was the real reason she'd hightailed it out of her studio and made a beeline for his house, despite the fact she could have easily worked for another three hours.

She wanted Nikos. At least, she amended silently, she wanted more of the incredible things he could do to her.

She smiled at him. "Well, I'm a little partial to your touch, too."

"Come with me," he said, and caught her hand.

Lexi was too surprised to protest as he pulled her out of the room and toward the staircase that led to the second floor. As far as she knew, the house was empty of furniture, so she couldn't imagine what he had in mind. At the top of the stairs, he drew her along the corridor and opened the door to the bathroom.

"I keep a few personal items here in case I need to clean up," he said, stepping back.

Lexi entered the bathroom and saw a stack of towels on the shelf and toiletries on the counter. A man's robe hung from a hook, and the room carried the scent that she had come to associate with Nikos—a mixture of spicy citrus and fresh cotton.

"You want me to shower here?" she asked in surprise.

"Why not? When you're finished, put on my robe and come downstairs. I'll make you dinner."

Lexi's eyebrows rose. "You keep enough supplies here to cook?"

Nikos shrugged. "Nothing fancy, just a cold salad."

Lexi hesitated. She'd come over here specifically to see Nikos, so what was the problem? Looking at him now, leaning negligently against the door frame of the small bathroom, she knew exactly what the problem was. She hadn't come over here for a shower and a cold salad, no matter how enticing both sounded. She wanted Nikos.

Naked.

Groaning.

Inside her.

"Maybe you could wash my back," she suggested softly.

She watched as heat flared in his eyes. Shrugging away

from the door frame, he stepped close and cupped her jaw in both hands. He rubbed a thumb across her lower lip.

"I'd love that," he assured her in a husky voice, his accent more pronounced. "But unfortunately, this shower won't fit two people. It's one of the first things I'm going to change when I renovate the bathroom. Take your shower, and then come downstairs."

He pressed a warm, moist kiss against her mouth, lingering for a long moment as she swayed against him. When he finally lifted his head, Lexi's knees felt a little wobbly. He left, closing the door behind him, and she sagged against the shower enclosure, disappointed. But when she pulled back the curtain, she saw he hadn't exaggerated. The space was tiny—too tiny for both of them.

Turning on the water, she quickly undressed, grimacing at the accumulation of dust on her clothing and skin. Stepping beneath the spray, she shampooed her hair and then quickly washed herself with his soap. There was something incredibly intimate about using his toiletries. As she turned the water off and dried herself with a thick towel, she realized she smelled like him.

Rubbing the condensation from the surface of the bathroom mirror, she inspected her reflection. Devoid of cosmetics, her skin was pale. She chewed her lips, hoping to pull some more color into them, and then pinched her cheeks. Sighing, she ran a comb through her hair. She'd never been the kind of woman who obsessed over her looks, but she wished now that she carried lip gloss or mascara in her purse. Of course, she could always run home and get dressed, but if she wore Nikos's bathrobe, as he'd suggested, she would be completely nude beneath the chocolate silk. Smiling in anticipation, she folded her discarded clothing into a neat pile, slipped into the robe and made her way downstairs. Nikos was in the kitchen with his back to her, working at the counter. As she padded silently toward him, he swore softly and put a finger to his mouth.

"Are you okay?" Lexi asked.

He spun around and his eyes swept over her. Lexi could see from his expression that he approved. He gave her a rueful smile. "I'm fine, just a nick."

Frowning, Lexi took his hand in hers and inspected the small slice on the side of his index finger. "You should run this under some water. Do you have any Band-Aids?"

Nikos nodded toward a cupboard. "I keep a first-aid kit in there."

As he washed the cut, Lexi pulled the kit down and found a bandage and some antiseptic. "Here, let me," she said when he reached for the items.

She applied some ointment before carefully wrapping his finger in the bandage. She didn't immediately release him. His hands were strong, the fingers lean and tapered and the nails clean and neat. Funny how much you could tell about a person from their hands. They were one of the first things that Lexi noticed when she met someone. That, and their teeth. Nikos had good teeth, as strong and well kept as his hands.

"I think you'll survive," she said, smiling at him.

He raised her hand to his lips. "Thank you."

Lexi knew she shouldn't feel so delighted each time he made a gallant gesture. After all, he was European and everyone knew European men were naturally charming. At least, that's what she'd heard. He was certainly more charming than any of the other men she'd been involved with.

"What are you making?" she asked when he released her hand.

He gestured for her to see for herself, and Lexi approached the counter. He had prepared two bowls, but what he claimed was nothing fancy was cold pasta salad with shrimp, cherry tomatoes, feta and basil. Her mouth began to water as she realized how hungry she was.

"Mmm, this looks delicious!"

"I am glad you approve. Why don't we eat in the sunroom."

Without waiting for her response, he scooped up both dishes and made his way to the far side of the house. Lexi followed him, and stopped on the threshold, momentarily speechless. The small room overlooked the valley, and with the sun just setting over the ocean, the view was breathtaking. In the time that it had taken Lexi to shower, Nikos had brought the small patio table and chairs indoors. He had found several half-spent candles and placed them on a dish in the center of the table beside a bottle of wine, two glasses and a baguette of crunchy bread.

Lexi turned to him. "When you said you brought a few things back, I didn't realize..."

"I wanted the option of inviting you to stay here," he said, giving her a lopsided grin.

Setting the salads down on the table, he held her chair out for her, and then moved to a windowsill where Lexi saw an iPod music system. Nikos scanned through the playlist, and soon the romantic strains of a Frank Sinatra song filled the room. He turned to Lexi and arched an eyebrow, silently asking if she approved.

"Very nice," she acknowledged. "But won't the home owners object to you using their house as your own personal love shack?"

She'd only meant to tease him, and was surprised when he sat down across from her, his expression puzzled.

"I thought you knew," he said, uncorking the bottle of wine and pouring some into her glass.

"Knew what?"

He filled his own glass and then lifted it to hers in a toast. "I *am* the home owner."

7

"SO, YOU ACTUALLY BOUGHT THIS house?" Lexi asked carefully.

Nikos nodded and tore the end off the baguette. "I did."

She gave a huff of laughter. "But how? I mean, this house listed for over a million dollars. Wait. Did your company purchase the house for you to restore and resell? I mean, it's not really yours, is it?"

Nikos frowned. "Why do you look so surprised? I assure you the house belongs to me."

He could see her struggling to form a response, and knew without her having to say anything that she had believed him to be no more than a day laborer, even though he'd told her what he did for a living. He took a sip of wine, but found he was no longer hungry. How many times in his life had people looked at him and believed him to be nothing more than an attractive facade without much going on inside? Despite the fact he had built a career and a comfortable life for himself, and had nothing to prove to anyone, he found it still irritated him.

"I'm just surprised, that's all," Lexi finally said. "I assumed that someone else had purchased the property and you were just the carpenter." She winced. "I didn't mean that the way it sounded. Obviously you're more than just a carpenter—you're an artist. The way that I'm an artist. We just work with different mediums."

Nikos grunted and took a forkful of salad, but he barely tasted the shrimp and pasta. He told himself that he wouldn't read too much into her reaction. She'd jumped to the same conclusion about him that dozens of other people before her had. He should be used to it by now. When she reached across the table and covered her hand with his, he went still. Looking up, he saw the distress in her dark eyes.

"I'm sorry," she said. "I've offended you, and I didn't mean to. Try to understand. The first time I saw you, you were swinging a hammer. You drive a pickup truck. You wear paint-covered jeans and a baseball cap." She gave him a smile. "Call me narrow-minded, but you don't exactly fit the stereotype of a wealthy home owner."

Nikos sighed and squeezed her fingers. "I'm not offended. And I haven't always had the means to purchase and restore properties like this one. But that's a story for another day." He raised his glass and forced a smile. "Here's a toast to being…neighborly."

Lexi took a sip of the chilled wine, but Nikos could almost hear the wheels turning in her head. She wanted to know what he had done before he came to California, but he wasn't interested in talking about his past. At least not tonight. Maybe one day, but not now. He was grateful that his modeling career had provided him with the means to come to California and start a new life, but when he thought about what he had sacrificed, he wondered if it had been worth it. The day his father had put him on that plane to London, he'd lost everything that had been important to him—his home, his family, his friends, and whatever had remained of his childhood.

Finding Lexi Adams had been an unexpected surprise.

She didn't seem interested in acquiring the material things that other women craved. Granted, she had slept with him based solely on her physical attraction to him, without knowing the first thing about him, but he was guilty of the same thing. He found himself thinking about Lexi when they weren't together, though. He didn't care what her motives were for sleeping with him; for the first time since he left Syros, he felt happy. Really, truly happy.

He watched as she took a forkful of the shrimp and pasta and then closed her eyes in sublime satisfaction. "Oh, this is delicious," she said, looking at him. "I can't believe you made it."

"I'm glad you like it."

"I love it. And the wine is perfect." She took a sip and then paused, looking at him. "How did you know that I would come over here tonight?"

"I didn't, but I hoped you would," he admitted.

Which was an understatement.

As soon as he'd left her house that morning, he'd driven straight to his home on Cliff Drive and loaded some items into the bed of his pickup truck, including a box of dishes and cooking utensils, his toiletries and several changes of clothes, a mattress and some bedding. If his cousins thought it unusual that he'd decided to move into the house, they hadn't said anything. He wasn't sure he'd even be able to explain his reasons; he just knew that he needed to be near Lexi, and there was no way he was going to drive to his beachfront home each night, not when she was in the house next door.

"I'm glad I did," she said simply.

Nikos watched as she ate her salad. Outside, the sun was dropping behind the horizon and the flickering candlelight cast a warm glow over her skin. She looked incredibly sexy in his silk robe, with her damp hair in tendrils around her face. He wondered if she wore anything beneath the silk, or if she was nude. Just the thought of her smooth, bare skin caused his body to harden, and he shifted uncomfortably.

She pushed her salad around and gave him a cautious look. "So I'm curious…what did you do before you came to the States? You said you left Syros when you were fourteen. Where were you between then, and when you came to California?"

Nikos hesitated and swirled his drink, considering his words. "I lived in London," he finally said. He didn't like to talk about those years, or his own feelings of abandonment. Realistically, he knew his parents had wanted him to go to London because there were more opportunities there than on the island of Syros, but he still harbored feelings of resentment that they had sent him away when he hadn't wanted to leave.

"Did your family move there?"

"No. Just me. I, um, studied there."

"Oh. That explains it."

Nikos sharpened his attention on her. "Explains what?"

"Your accent. Sometimes it has an almost British ring to it."

Nikos relaxed fractionally. He didn't want to talk about those days. When people discovered he had been a top model, they invariably looked at him differently. Many did an internet search of his name and were shocked by what they saw. For himself, he never looked at those ads and he kept no reminders of that time, with the possible exception of his comfortable bank account. He preferred to market himself as a master carpenter and a restoration specialist for historic homes.

Turn-of-the-century arts-and-crafts-style bungalows were his specialty, and there was no shortage of them in Santa Barbara. Soon, he'd established a reputation, and now he found he could pick and choose his jobs. It was a good place to be. He no longer identified with the idealistic, naive young man who had walked the catwalks of London, Paris and Milan, and had starred in provocative advertising campaigns with some of the most stunning women in the world. Those experiences belonged to another person, in another lifetime. Given a choice, he'd much rather be here with Lexi. With her damp hair and freshly scrubbed face, she was a thousand times more attractive to him than the supermodels he had once worked with.

He indicated her half-eaten salad. "Are you finished? You didn't have much."

She looked at him, amused. "You didn't eat at all."

Pushing his salad aside, he leaned forward and laced his fingers with hers on the tabletop. "I'm not hungry. At least, not for food."

Before she could respond, he released her hand and stood up to carry their dishes through the house and into the kitchen. With the sun setting, the house was dim and cool with deepening shadows, and Nikos didn't bother to switch on any of the overhead lights. "It's a beautiful night. Why don't I grab a blanket, and we can go outside and enjoy the view."

He stacked the bowls on the counter, but didn't hear her follow him on bare feet. He didn't know she was there until she slid her arms around him, pressing herself against his back and splaying her hands over his chest and stomach.

"At the risk of sounding rude, I'm not interested in going outside," she said softly. "Not when the view in here is so much better."

Her hands stroked over his torso, and Nikos barely suppressed a groan at the sensation of her warm palms through the thin cotton of his shirt. He turned around and leaned against the counter. She tipped her head back to look at him, her eyes filled with suggestion. Her hair was drying in soft waves around her shoulders and her skin had a faint flush of color.

"What did you have in mind?"

Lexi smiled and slid her hands beneath the hem of his shirt. Her fingers stroked over his skin, and suddenly the room felt overly warm.

"I was thinking of dessert, actually," she said, pushing the fabric upward. She leaned forward and pressed warm, moist lips to the center of his chest, before licking him lightly. "Mmm. Delicious."

Framing her face in his hands, Nikos studied her. Her mouth was lush and pliant, and with a soft groan, he bent and covered it with his own. She responded instantly, pressing herself against him and sliding her hands to his back and then lower to cup his butt and urge him closer. He broke free just long enough to drag his shirt over his head and drop it onto the floor before Lexi pushed him back against the counter and resumed her sensual assault.

"You taste so good," she breathed, dragging her mouth along the length of his neck and collarbone.

Nikos sucked in air and tried to focus, but it was impossible with her hands and mouth on him. He'd spent most of the day thinking about her and replaying their night together. Then, during dinner, he'd found himself fantasizing about what she might—or might not—be wearing beneath his bathrobe. But when her fingers went to the button on his waistband, a small vestige of sanity resurfaced and he caught her wrists.

"Do you really want to do this here?" he asked, his voice rough with arousal.

But Lexi merely smiled. "Oh, yeah. I've been thinking about this all day."

Keeping her eyes on his face, she unfastened the button

on his jeans and slowly drew the zipper down. Her eyes grew heated as she slipped her hand inside and cupped his rigid length. Her breath slipped out on a soft sigh of appreciation as she stroked him.

Nikos gripped the edge of the counter and watched as she hooked her thumbs into the waistband of his jeans and slowly pushed them down over his thighs. His erection stood out stiffly from his body, and when Lexi dropped to her knees in front of him and curled her hands around his length, he thought he would lose it right then and there.

"Lexi," he groaned. "Maybe we should take this somewhere more private."

In answer, she looked up at him briefly before returning her attention to his twitching cock. "Why? It's just the two of us. Nobody can see."

Before he had time to think of a reason why they shouldn't do this, she drew her tongue along his length. A shudder went through him, and then he ceased to think altogether.

Lexi rocked back on her heels and her gaze traveled over him. Nikos could see the feminine appreciation in her eyes and felt himself grow even harder. He gripped the counter and struggled for control.

"You are so beautiful," Lexi whispered, and leaned forward to take him in her mouth. He groaned deeply as she suckled him, running her tongue around the corona and then drawing on him like a Popsicle. Her mouth was hot and slick, and when she wrapped one hand around the base of his shaft and squeezed, he thought he would come undone. With her free hand, she stroked his bare thigh before cupping his balls and rolling them gently in her palm. Nikos gave a deep sigh of pleasure and released the counter to bury his hands in her hair. His fingertips traced the contours of her ears and jaw as she drew on him. Finally, when he could stand no more, he told her to stop, but she didn't reply. He was only vaguely aware that he'd reverted to his native Greek. He gripped her by the upper arms and hauled her to her feet.

"If you don't stop," he rasped in English, "I am not going to last."

"I don't want you to—" She didn't get to finish her sentence as Nikos grabbed her face and kissed her hard and deep, spearing his tongue against hers and feasting on her mouth. Without breaking the kiss, he slid his hands down the length of her back and cupped her buttocks in his hands, lifting her against him. Lexi moaned her approval and wound her arms around his neck as he turned and set her down on the edge of the kitchen counter, shoving dishes aside in his haste.

"Oh, thank Christ," he breathed as he opened the front of her robe. She was nude beneath the silk, as he'd wanted her to be. Her breasts rose and fell rapidly with her agitated breathing, and her nipples were erect, begging for his touch. "You are naked."

"I was hoping you'd notice," Lexi said coyly, slanting him a provocative smile, and then gasped as he cupped both breasts in his hands and leaned forward to press his mouth against the side of her neck. She speared her fingers through his hair as he lowered his head to one breast and drew a nipple into his mouth. He laved her with his tongue, flicking the distended tip until she arched against him and gripped his hips with her thighs. But when he eased a hand between their bodies and stroked her intimately, Lexi mewled with pleasure and widened her legs to give him better access.

"You're so ready for me," he groaned, swirling a finger through her dampness.

"I want you inside me," she said breathlessly. "Now."

Without answering, Nikos bent down and fumbled through his jean pockets for his wallet. Pulling it out, he withdrew two condoms. "I picked some up this morning, just in case."

"Smart man," Lexi said. "Here, let me."

Opening one of the foil packets, she covered him quickly with hands that trembled. Nikos pulled her to the edge of the counter, and she moaned softly as he pressed himself against the most intimate part of her and then, sweet, blessed Mary, he was pushing himself into her welcoming moistness.

She gasped and hooked her heels around his thighs as she met the thrusts of his tongue against hers with equal urgency. God, she felt incredible, all slick heat and pulsating tightness. He grasped her hips in his hands and thrust himself into her, knowing he wasn't being gentle, but beyond the point where he could restrain himself. She welcomed him just as fiercely, gripping his hips tightly with her thighs and using her heels to urge him deeper. Her fingers tunneled through his hair and she moaned into his mouth, making small sounds of pleasure and rising need.

He dragged his mouth from hers. "I want to see you," he growled, and lowered his forehead to hers, watching himself surge into her. Her nipples were tightly erect, straining toward him. With a groan, he drew one into his mouth, suckling her hard. She cried out and arched her back, and he felt her tightening around him, gripping and squeezing him until, with a harsh cry, he climaxed in a powerful surge of exquisite pleasure.

For several long moments, there was only the sound of their harsh breathing. Nikos knew he should pull away, but his body wouldn't obey. For the first time since he'd left the island of Syros, he felt as if he'd finally come home.

8

SEX. SCULPTURE. NIKOS.

Over the course of three weeks, Lexi's world had been reduced to these three realities, and they blurred into each other so that she was no longer certain where one began and the other ended. One thing *was* certain: she'd become an addict. When she wasn't actually having sex with Nikos, she was consumed with thoughts of having sex with him. Even the time spent in her studio, away from him, didn't provide a reprieve since she was essentially sculpting Nikos, which only led to more thoughts of sex with him.

Somehow, Lexi managed to get herself to her studio and put in ten to twelve hours of solid work each day. By rights, she should be exhausted, and while there were times when she got home and fell into bed, it definitely wasn't so that she could sleep. Essentially, when she wasn't working, she was having sex with Nikos.

She didn't want to think too much about what she was doing, or what she was getting herself involved in. She wasn't sure she could explain it, even to herself. She and Nikos had never gone out in public, and she hadn't told anyone about him. They were lovers, certainly, and she hoped they were also friends. But she hesitated to think they were anything more than that. She told herself it was for the best, since Nikos had already informed her of his plan to sell the house once he completed the renovations. Beyond that, they hadn't talked about their future, but Lexi had no illusions that once his work was finished, he would stick around.

Her own work was progressing quickly. She had finished the head and face and sometimes she found herself just sitting, staring at what she'd created. The resemblance to Nikos was uncanny, and she'd exceeded her own expectations in capturing his likeness. She'd also completed most of his torso, and had begun defining his taut, muscular butt and manly parts. Maybe that was the reason she arrived home each night with sex on her mind.

She'd fallen into a habit of grabbing a quick shower before walking next door to see what transformation Nikos had accomplished in the house that day. Sometimes they would make love right away, urgently, as if they didn't have all night to enjoy each other. Other times, they would prepare a light dinner, either at his house or hers, before going upstairs to her bedroom. Lexi had never slept in Nikos's house. No matter how late she stayed, he always walked her home and then spent the night in her bed.

Lexi knew she was treading dangerous waters; she was at serious risk of falling for Nikos. The worst part was that she actually looked for flaws, but could find nothing. The guy was pretty damn close to perfect—not only gorgeous, but great in bed. She loved spending time with him. He had a wry sense of humor that appealed to her, and he could talk knowledgeably about any number of topics. He was hardworking and financially independent, and he seemed genuinely into her. So why did she feel as if she was always waiting for the other shoe to drop? She tried to keep an open mind about Nikos, but there was a little voice in the back of her head warning her not to get too attached. She'd only end up disappointed.

The days passed swiftly for Lexi, as if in a dream. Her entire world had become this man and her sculpture. Each night, Lexi would focus on one particular part of Nikos's body, memorizing the shape and texture of a limb, the sleekness and strength of a particular muscle, the thrust of his shoulders. The next morning, in her studio, she would draw on those sensual memories to slowly chip away at the sculpture and draw forth the strength and beauty of Apollo.

On the third weekend, they both took a break from work to spend the day together. They made leisurely love before Nikos went downstairs to make coffee. Wearing a robe over a pair of flannel shorts and a camisole, Lexi joined him in the sunroom. He'd found a soft-jazz station on the radio, and a tray of breakfast pastries stood on the coffee table alongside two steaming mugs.

"Mmm, this is nice," she commented, but her eyes were on Nikos, who lounged on the big sofa with his legs stretched out in front of him. He wore a T-shirt and a pair of shorts, and his bare skin gleamed warm and brown in the sunlight that slanted through the big windows.

"This is my favorite room," he said. "Come here." He patted the cushion beside him, but when she went to sit down, he swung his legs up on the sofa and dragged her close, until she lay sprawled with her back resting against his chest. "Much better."

Reaching over, he picked up a mug of coffee and handed it to her. Lexi leaned back against him, feeling his chest fall and rise. His legs bracketed hers, and she admired their long, muscular length, unable to resist rubbing her foot against his ankle.

"I brought the paper in," he said, and indicated the newspaper that lay on the table next to the pastries.

"Oh, good. There's an article about the new Garden of the Gods at the botanic gardens." Lexi reached for the paper. "I hope they took a picture of Poseidon."

As she unfolded the arts section, Nikos rested his chin on her shoulder so that they could read the piece together. A color photograph of Poseidon took up nearly the entire page.

"You did this?" Nikos asked in astonishment as he studied the picture.

"I did." Lexi felt absurdly pleased by his surprise. "Do you like it?"

Nikos slid an arm around her waist as he pressed a kiss against her neck. "I think it's magnificent. I feel humbled to be in the presence of such a talented artist."

Lexi pinched his thigh. "Now you're teasing me."

Laughing, he tilted her head so that he could kiss her mouth. "Maybe about the humble part," he murmured against her lips, "but I am being sincere when I say that the sculpture is amazing. I can't believe how real he looks. I think we need to visit the gardens so that I can see it up close."

For Lexi, she could think of no greater compliment, and she felt a profound sense of pleasure that Nikos appreciated her work.

"Wait until you see the piece I'm working on right now," she enthused. "I think this may be my best work yet."

"When will it be finished?"

"Soon. As much as I complain about the long hours you spend working on your house, it's forced me to spend an equal amount of time in my studio." She smiled. "Not that it's a hardship. I've never felt so inspired. At this rate, I'll deliver the sculpture weeks ahead of schedule."

"When can I see it?"

"When it's delivered to the gardens and not a day

sooner," she said. Turning her face, she pressed a kiss against the corner of his mouth to take the sting out of her words. "I hope you don't mind."

Nikos shrugged. "Of course not. Every artist has their own process. You like to work in solitude. There's nothing wrong with that, it's just the way it is."

Lexi looked at him, surprised by his perception. She did require solitude when she worked. She hated for anyone to see her work before it was completed, and even when she left each evening, she was careful to conceal her project beneath a dust cloth.

"What's your process?" she asked, folding the newspaper and setting it on the floor. "When you're restoring an old house? Do you prefer to work alone?"

"Just the opposite," he remarked. "I like to have people around. I need to hear how the rooms absorb and project sound, see how traffic flows and determine where the heart of the house is located. I can't do that if I'm by myself."

Nikos didn't talk much about his work, although Lexi had seen for herself the skill, craftsmanship and innate sense of style that he possessed. In the few weeks that they had known each other, he and his cousins had almost completely restored the downstairs of the house next door. As he had promised, he had stripped the paint from the existing woodwork and the results were stunning. Where the original built-in cabinetry had long ago been ripped out, Nikos had built new cabinetry, and that was where his skill was most evident, at least to Lexi.

The only room on the first floor that remained unfinished was the kitchen, and Nikos had been searching for appliances that would meet the demands of a modern family, while still preserving the authenticity of the original house. Meanwhile, his cousins had almost completely restored the exterior, and Nikos had brought in several subcontractors to landscape the yard and make repairs to the swimming pool. The house was quickly turning into a showpiece, and Lexi had no doubt that he would make a killing when it finally went on the market.

"How did you get involved in restoring older homes?" she asked as she sipped her coffee.

"As a boy, I worked with my father and uncles. They owned a construction business and did repairs and renovations on some of the older homes on Syros. I enjoyed the work, and I was happy to rediscover it when I came here."

He grew silent, and Lexi knew he was remembering those days when he had lived on the island. She had never asked him about his childhood, sensing it wasn't a topic he cared to discuss. But neither did he like to talk about the time he had spent in London, and Lexi realized that even after three weeks, she knew only a little more about Nikos than she had on the day she first met him.

"Does your father still live in Greece?" she asked cautiously.

"Yes. He's retired now, but my brothers and cousins have kept the business going."

"You have brothers?" Lexi asked in surprise, her imagination running riot.

"Three brothers and two sisters."

Lexi digested this information, envisioning a family of almost surreal beauty. She hoped she never received an invitation to a family gathering, because if his siblings were as gorgeous as Nikos, she wouldn't survive the introductions without making a slobbering fool of herself.

"Do they look anything like you?" she asked.

"There's definitely a family resemblance," he said, amused. "I have a picture of them in my wallet that I can show you."

"Oh, yes, I want to see it. Where's your wallet?"

"I think I left it on your bedside table."

Lexi jumped up. "I'll go get it."

She ran lightly up the stairs, eager to see the photo. Nikos rarely talked about himself, so offering to show her a picture of his family was huge, and Lexi admitted that she was more than a little curious about his past. She wanted to know everything about him. Grabbing his wallet from the night table, she brought it back downstairs and handed it to him before climbing back onto the couch and leaning against him.

Offering an amused look, Nikos opened the wallet and withdrew a photo that was creased and dog-eared with age and handling. "This was taken just before I went to London. I was fourteen."

Taking the photo from him, Lexi studied it. She had no trouble spotting Nikos among the six children, and her breath caught at how beautiful he'd been as a teenager. He was right about his siblings; they were all stunning. She could see the resemblance to his father, who looked like a slightly older, more rugged version of Nikos. His mother was tiny by comparison, but Nikos had her eyes.

"Do they all still live in Greece? I mean, do they ever come to California?"

"They still live on Syros, but everyone's been to the States, except for my father. Why do you ask?"

"Because I can't imagine why a modeling scout hasn't found you before now," she said, only half joking. "There's this family of pig farmers in Nebraska, and the sons look like Viking gods. They were discovered years ago by a top modeling agent, and let's just say that they now have the financial means to do just about anything they want."

"And do they?"

Lexi gave him a wry smile. "No. They went back to pig farming."

"Not everyone is looking for fame and fortune."

"I guess not," Lexi acknowledged. "Although fame and fortune would certainly make life a lot easier."

"Or a lot more complicated."

"What do you mean?"

"I think people with money always have to be on their guard."

Lexi looked at him speculatively. "You sound as if you're speaking from personal experience."

Nikos was quiet for several long minutes. He stroked her arm with the backs of his fingers, but Lexi could see his thoughts were elsewhere.

"Is your family wealthy?" she finally asked, because she could think of no other reason for his words. He'd grown up on Syros, had gone to school in London. Maybe his family had money.

Nikos gave a bark of laughter. "Good God, no. My family is definitely working class. My father was a builder with six children at home, and my mother didn't work, at least not outside the house. Trust me, there was no extra money."

"So how could you afford to go to school in England?"

He was silent for several long moments, and then blew out a resigned breath. "I didn't actually go to school," he finally said. "You joke about it, but when I was fourteen I was discovered by a modeling agent. My father sent me to London in the belief that I'd have a better life than the one he could give me."

Lexi was shocked. There was no doubt that Nikos had striking good looks, but she couldn't envision him posing in front of a camera. He seemed too private for that. "You were really a model?"

"I was."

"Did someone go with you?"

"No. I went by myself."

"Were you successful?" She'd never paid much attention to fashion, and if Nikos had been fourteen when he'd started, that would have been eighteen years ago.

Nikos laughed softly. "Not right away."

Lexi tried to imagine what it must have been like for him, a teenage boy, with no family and no support system, trying to make a living in a foreign country. "Did you even speak English?"

"Yes, but not very well."

"Where did you live? Who took care of you? Did you go to school?"

Nikos hugged her against his chest. "It was a long time ago. None of that matters anymore."

Lexi twisted so she could see his face. "It matters to me. Please tell me you weren't alone."

He gave her a wry smile. "I lived in an apartment with seven other boys, all trying to break into the business. We spent our days going to casting calls, and if we were lucky enough to get selected, then we'd attend fittings, photo shoots and shows. It was hard work, and for those first few years I barely had enough money to pay the rent."

Lexi stared at him, shocked. "The modeling agent who discovered you brought you all the way to London and then expected you to immediately support yourself?"

He shrugged. "That's the way the business goes. I paid twelve hundred dollars a month for a metal bunk bed in a crappy apartment, and if I couldn't find work then I was out on the street."

"But you were only fourteen!"

"The other boys in the apartment were around the same age." He laughed softly. "Christ, when I think back on those days…it's amazing I survived that first year."

"Did you find work right away?"

"The agency lined up casting calls every day, and I

was usually selected for fittings or photo shoots, but even then it was tough."

"How so?"

He gave a laugh. "In the beginning, I was paid next to nothing per shoot, or compensated with clothing. It's a little hard to pay the rent with a retro peacoat or a pair of designer blue jeans."

Lexi considered his words. "I can't imagine how difficult that must have been. Did you go to school, or did you have a tutor?"

Nikos carefully disentangled himself from her and stood up, rolling his shoulders as he walked over to the windows and stared through them, although Lexi was sure he didn't even see the magnificent view. Setting her coffee down, she went to stand beside him.

"I didn't go to school while I was in England," he said. "At first, I didn't have time for studies, except for a tutor to help me improve my English. Later, I had no desire to go back to school. I was doing well financially, and I was too young and too arrogant to believe I could benefit from an education." He glanced at her. "I eventually went back and passed my exams, but if I could do it over again, I'd make some better choices."

"Is that why you never returned to Syros?" she asked quietly. "Because your modeling career was so successful?"

She saw the regret in his eyes. "No. In the beginning, I didn't go back because I couldn't afford the airfare. Even if I could have, I was too angry at my father for having sent me away. Later, I didn't go back because I didn't want my family to see what I'd become."

Lexi frowned. "What do you mean? You've made a success of yourself. I'm sure your parents are very proud of you."

Nikos gave her a wry smile. "I've been out of the modeling business for more than eight years, but I'm not sure that's enough time for my father to forget some of the things I did. He came to London once, when I was sixteen. He showed up unexpectedly on the set of a shoot I was doing for an underwear campaign." He scrubbed a hand across his face. "He was so outraged that he tried to drag me out of the studio and force me to come home with him."

Lexi might not know much about fashion, but she had seen some of the full-page ad campaigns in magazines and knew they could be provocative. She was certain that even her overdeveloped imagination didn't come close to what Nikos's father must have seen that day on the set.

"What happened?"

Nikos grimaced in memory. "We had this huge argument, right there in the studio, and he ended up leaving without me."

"I'm sorry. That must have been awful."

"It was. I blamed him. You see, I'd had no interest in becoming a model. I'd wanted to stay on Syros, with my family and friends. But the agent made everything sound so wonderful, like a dream. In the end, my father insisted that I go with her and I never really forgave him for that. I told him that if he didn't like what I was doing, he only had himself to blame."

Lexi stared at him, comprehension beginning to dawn. "Are you telling me that you haven't seen your father since you were sixteen?"

Nikos looked at her, his eyes troubled. "I've never been able to forget the disappointment on his face the last time I saw him. How could I ever face him again?"

"Nikos, you were just a kid! Surely he understood that what you were doing was part of a business? I doubt he holds that against you. But Nikos…to stay away for eighteen years?"

"There were other reasons, things I can't talk about."

Lexi heard the self-loathing in his voice and could only guess at what he referred to. She tried to imagine what it must have been like to be a young man with no parental supervision in a foreign country surrounded by so much temptation and opportunity. Her own stomach tensed at the thought of what he might have been exposed to, but she also recognized that those experiences, good and bad, had made him the man he was today. She found it hard to believe that his father wouldn't be proud of who he had become.

"Nikos, he's your father. Whatever you've done in your life, I'm sure he would forgive you." Grasping his hands, she turned him to face her. "Listen to me. I lost my parents five years ago. They were killed in a pileup on Highway 99 south of Fresno. Don't you think I would give anything to have them back?" She gestured to the view outside the windows. "I'd gladly give up all this to have them here. I'd live in a crappy one-room apartment in the worst part of town if it meant I could come back here and visit them. So to think that you've deliberately shut your parents out of your life is just…well, it's incomprehensible to me."

"Lexi, you don't know the kind of person I was then."

"That doesn't matter now. Like I said, you were just a kid."

"And what about later? When I was in my twenties? The kind of lifestyle I led…" He scrubbed his hands over his face.

"What made you finally give it up?" Lexi asked.

Nikos blew out a hard breath. "I can't believe I'm telling you this. I've never talked about it with anyone."

Lexi hugged him. The pain and vulnerability she saw on

his face made her want to protect him. At the same time, she realized that she'd been wrong to believe she could get involved with Nikos and keep her emotions separate. She was already in over her head. "You can tell me anything," she said. "My feelings for you aren't going to change."

"By the time I was twenty-three, I had my own place that I shared with my friend Erik, another model. But where I had gained success, he was starting to lose work. He hadn't been signed for anything in months and had almost no money left, but I was the only one who knew that. He had a beautiful girlfriend who seemed to be crazy about him. I think he would have married her, but she found out about his financial situation and left him. It seems she was only interested in models with lucrative campaigns."

"That's terrible."

"It was. Eric was devastated. At the same time, both of us were under consideration to become the face of a leading men's fragrance. I didn't really need the work or the money, but Eric did. When they selected me, I should have done the right thing and declined the contract, but I didn't."

"That's called business, Nikos. You can't be blamed for the company choosing you over your roommate."

Nikos's lips twisted. "He didn't see it that way. But when his girlfriend started to come around again, I thought she was interested in getting back together with him, but it seems she was interested in me, instead. Eric came home and found us alone together. I never touched her, and I swore to him that I wasn't interested in her, but he didn't believe me."

"What happened?"

"A few days later, he took his own life."

Lexi gasped and instinctively grasped his hand, trying to give him reassurance and comfort. "That wasn't your fault, Nikos."

"Maybe not, but it opened my eyes. I began to see people for who they really were and I realized that it wasn't me they were interested in as much as what I could do for them. Erik's death also put things into perspective for me. I wanted to do something meaningful with my life, not just look attractive."

"That must have been tough."

"It was a hard lesson. I wanted to complete the contracts I had, but I was so disillusioned that I knew I needed to get out. I thought I was the one being taken advantage of, but I realized that I wasn't much better—to a certain extent, I used my looks and my success to take advantage of others. I didn't like the person I'd become, so I left modeling and came to California."

"So that's why you wouldn't model for me," she said in understanding.

"I'm sorry about that. I made a promise to myself a long time ago that I would never model again, under any circumstances."

Lexi thought about the statue of Apollo in her studio. She knew she should tell Nikos that she had already carved the sculpture in his image, but wondered how he would feel about that. What if he told her he didn't want his face on the statue? She would have to start all over again. But since she'd met Nikos, she couldn't envision the sculpture having any other face.

"Are any of your photos still used in advertising?" she asked cautiously.

His eyebrows drew together. "No. The rights ran out about three years ago. If anyone uses my image now, in any capacity, I think I'd have to sue them. My days of being a commodity for others to profit from are over."

Lexi felt her heart drop into her stomach at his words. She should tell him about the sculpture; he would understand. When she'd created Apollo in his image, she hadn't known about his past, or how he felt about modeling. But she was a coward. She crossed her arms over her middle and stared out the window, knowing that she wouldn't say anything. But she also knew that when he finally did see the sculpture of Apollo, she might never see Nikos again.

9

"WHY ARE YOU LETTING ME SEE the sculpture now before it's even finished?"

"Just keep your eyes closed, and don't open them until I tell you to," Lexi instructed. Keeping her hand over her friend's eyes, she led Nelda through her studio to a chair and pushed her down onto it. "No peeking."

Nelda gave an exaggerated sigh. "I promise."

Drawing a deep breath, Lexi pulled the dust sheet off the statue. "Okay, you can look."

Nelda opened her eyes, blinking a little at the bright sunlight pouring through the windows. Then her gaze fastened on the sculpture and her mouth opened. As if in a trance, she rose to her feet and walked over to stand before it.

"Oh, my God," she breathed, staring up at the face. At Nikos's face. "He's the perfect man."

Lexi stood a few feet away, hands clasped in front of her. "I still have some more work to do refining and polishing the details, but to all intents and purposes, it's done. What do you think?" She gave her friend a timid but hopeful smile.

Nelda let out an exhale of breath and gave Lexi a disbelieving look. “Are you *kidding?* Lexi, this is—” She broke off in astonished laughter. “I thought Poseidon was freaking hot, but this guy is unbelievable!” She circled the sculpture, letting her fingers trail over muscle and sinew, lingering a little too long on the hard curve of a buttock.

“So…you like it?”

“Like it?” Nelda’s eyes devoured the figure of Apollo. “I want to take him home with me. I mean, look at this guy.” As if to emphasize her words, she put her hand over his crotch, playfully cupping his manly parts. “What I couldn’t do with this.” She slanted Lexi an amused glance. “Is this the reason I haven’t seen you for weeks and weeks? Because you’ve been too busy with your new boy toy here?”

Lexi thought guiltily of Nikos and how she’d spent every spare moment in his company. She’d had plenty of time to visit Nelda or take a drive into downtown Santa Barbara to stop by her gallery, but the truth was that she didn’t want to do anything that interfered with the time she spent with Nikos.

“Yes,” she said, only half fibbing. “I usually spend ten to twelve hours a day here, and when I get home I’m too beat to do much else.”

Except spend the night worshipping Nikos, her own personal Greek god. In the weeks since he’d told her about the falling-out he’d had with his father and the death of his friend, he had worked on the house renovations with a renewed intensity, as if he had something to prove. He’d hired additional workers, and now Lexi barely recognized the house next door. He’d turned it into a true showpiece. Even the yard had been transformed. He’d had the swimming pool custom tiled with Greek-key symbols around the edge, and at the bottom of the deep end was a mosaic of dolphins. A pergola had been raised on the spot where they had shared lunch that first day, and flowering shrubs and trees were planted strategically around the property.

Inside, the transformation was complete. Nikos had spared no expense. He'd even hired an event planner to assist him in hosting an open house to celebrate the completion of the restoration and to attract potential buyers. The house hadn't gone on the market yet, and already he was receiving offers.

"How can you bear to give him up?" Nelda asked. "I swear, I want to hold a mirror under his nose to make sure he's not breathing. He's so realistic, it's a little unnerving."

"Do you think so?"

"Oh, yeah." Tilting her head, Nelda surveyed the sculpture with a critical eye. "When are you turning it over to the botanic gardens?"

"Not for another couple of weeks. I'm ahead of schedule and they're not expecting delivery until next month."

Nelda eyed the sculpture with an expression of longing. "I'd love to display him before he gets shipped off to the gardens."

Lexi didn't say anything, but knew she could never put the sculpture in Nelda's gallery. She wasn't even sure she should turn the piece over to the art association. Averting her gaze, she murmured something noncommittal, hoping Nelda wouldn't pursue the subject.

"Who did you use as your model?" Nelda asked. "I swear, he reminds me of someone, I just can't think who."

"I actually used Nikos."

Nelda swung around, her expression one of astonishment. "The guy who took your camera? This is him? I mean, obviously you've embellished the details to make him seem more godly, but your scheme to have him model for you actually worked?"

"Um, as I recall, it was *your* scheme," Lexi reminded

her with a smile. "And no, it didn't work. He refused to sit for me, so I had to do the entire piece from memory. And I didn't embellish anything," she added smugly. "Everything is true to the original and in perfect proportion."

"Holy..." Nelda's voice trailed off as she turned her attention back to the sculpture with renewed interest. "So you're telling me that you and Nikos are—that you're together? As in, *together?*"

Lexi nodded, unable to keep the silly grin off her face. Even after two months, he still had the ability to make her feel like a teenager with her first crush, and her knees still went a little wobbly whenever he walked into a room. And the way he made love to her...

"Okay, there's no need to rub it in," Nelda said, watching Lexi's expression, but her smile said she was happy for her friend. "I can't believe you've been seeing him all this time and never said a word to me about it!"

"Well, I've hardly seen you."

"What did you say his last name was?" Nelda was looking at the statue with a thoughtful expression on her face. "Christakos? Is that it?"

Dread fisted itself in Lexi's stomach. "Yes. That's his last name. Why? Do you know him?"

"He's a little hard to forget," Nelda said drily. "He comes into the gallery sometimes. He purchased a couple of paintings for his house earlier this year. I remember him now...green eyes, right? Drop-dead gorgeous?"

Lexi nodded. "That's him."

"So what does he think about the sculpture you did of him? You have to admit it's appropriate—Nikos Christakos as the sun god." She sighed dramatically.

"He doesn't know."

Nelda frowned. "How can he not know? You haven't told him?"

"No. I'm afraid of how he'll react."

Without going into too much detail about Nikos's past, Lexi explained to Nelda his dislike of modeling, and how he'd sworn never to let anyone profit from using his image.

"So if he finds out that I've sculpted Apollo in his likeness, I'm not sure how he'll react." Lexi sat down in the chair that Nelda had vacated and buried her face in her hands. "I should have told him earlier, and now it's too late. I've ruined everything. He's absolutely perfect, but when he finds out about this, he won't want anything more to do with me."

"Wait. Didn't you say that you'd almost finished the sculpture by the time he told you how he felt?"

Raising her head, Lexi nodded miserably. "Yes. But it doesn't matter. When I first asked him to model for me, he refused. It should have ended there."

"But he didn't model for you, and there's no law that says you can't use someone as a source of inspiration. Is there?"

Lexi gave her friend a tolerant look. "I think I went a little beyond inspiration, Nelda. Besides, I still have the photos I took of him that first day. I don't understand why he didn't just delete them from my camera when he had the chance."

"Maybe, on some level, he wanted you to have them and he knew you would use them." Nelda shrugged. "Either way, it doesn't matter. He didn't model for you and you're not going to profit from using his image. I'm assuming you already negotiated your commission for this piece before you started working on it, am I right?"

"Yes, that's true. I have a contract that was negotiated with the botanic gardens more than a year ago. Five years to sculpt five heroes for them."

Nelda looked triumphant. "So there you go! I don't see how he could be upset about the sculpture. It's not like you deliberately deceived him."

Lexi frowned, unconvinced. "Maybe not, but my moral meter is still flashing red." She groaned. "How am I going to tell him the truth?"

"I think you're worrying for no reason," Nelda said. "The sculpture is fabulous, and I'm sure he'll be flattered and thrilled to know you modeled it after him."

Lexi wasn't convinced. "I don't know. I should probably negotiate a new delivery date with the art association and send them something else—a sculpture of Zeus or Hermes. I'm thinking I might just keep this piece here in the studio."

Nelda looked horrified. "You would do that? Even if it means losing months of work and having to start all over again?"

Lexi looked at the sculpture and silently acknowledged that she might lose more than just the months of hard work she'd devoted to the project. She might very well lose Nikos.

Now she nodded. "Yes."

Nelda was silent for several moments. "Well, I think it would be a shame to let such a magnificent piece sit here under a shroud, when so many people could enjoy its beauty."

Silently, Lexi agreed. But she knew now that she couldn't put the statue on display without Nikos's permission. She just wished she knew how he would react.

Reading her thoughts, Nelda walked over and gave her a sympathetic hug. "I'm sure it will work out," she said. "But if it doesn't, try to look on the bright side." She glanced meaningfully at the sculpture. "If all else fails, you'll still have the world's most perfect man."

As soon as the house sold, Nikos determined that he would return to Syros. Lexi had been right about one thing—life was too short to waste on anger and regret. He missed his family home. He missed his parents. Whatever his father's motives had been in sending him to London all those years ago, Nikos knew they had come from his heart and from a true desire to improve his son's life. And Nikos had managed to do that.

He hadn't told Lexi, but he already had a potential buyer for the house; a Hollywood director who was looking for a place to raise his young family. He'd made Nikos an exorbitant offer, but Nikos hadn't yet accepted it. The property was listed in several exclusive magazines, and his real estate agent had convinced him to have an open house the following weekend to celebrate the completion of the renovations, and to attract even more interested buyers. It would be a gala event, and Nikos wanted Lexi there with him. Then later, when they were alone, he would ask her to come to Syros with him to meet his family.

When he thought about returning to his childhood home, he experienced both dread and anticipation. He'd seen his brothers and sisters during their trips to California, and his mother had come to visit him several times, both in England and in California. But he hadn't seen his father in sixteen years.

Now he walked through the rooms of the finished house, surveying his handiwork with a critical eye. He'd hired a professional staging consultant to furnish the place and showcase its unique features. Overall, he was more than satisfied with the finished product, but now that the work was completed, he was eager to move on. He disliked spending too much time on one project, and he had more important things to focus on.

Like Lexi.

He glanced at his watch. She should be home anytime now. He'd told her about the open house, and although she'd been enthusiastic about the event, he'd sensed a change in her over the past week. She was as sweet and passionate as she'd always been, but he'd sensed something else in their lovemaking—a desperation of sorts. She seemed preoccupied and there were times when he'd caught her watching him with a troubled expression, which she quickly concealed behind a smile. Something was bothering her, and he suspected it was the sale of the house. She probably thought that once the house sold, she wouldn't see him anymore.

She couldn't be more wrong.

He'd fallen hard for her. He intended to show her just what she meant to him during their trip to Syros. He'd also arranged for them to spend several days on the island of Santorini, since that was something she'd always wanted to do. They'd have to make some decisions about their future, but that could wait until they returned.

As if on cue, the front door opened, and Lexi poked her head inside. "Nikos, are you here?"

"In the living room," he called, and stepped into the hallway to meet her. "I was just wondering where you were."

"Sorry." She smiled, reaching up to press a kiss against his mouth. "I had a visitor at the studio this afternoon and ended up staying a little longer than I intended."

Nikos leaned back to study her face. "You let someone into your studio? Does that mean what I think it means?"

To his surprise, Lexi withdrew from his arms and walked into the living room, looking around as if she hadn't already seen the furniture that had been brought in for the open house.

"Yes," she said over her shoulder. "Except for the final polishing, the sculpture is finished."

Nikos welcomed the news, even as he wondered why she hadn't said anything about it before now. He wanted to leave for Syros as soon as possible after the open house, and hopefully after he'd signed the deal. He'd been waiting for Lexi to complete her project so that they could both enjoy their time together without any deadlines hanging over their heads.

"Why didn't you tell me you were so close to finishing it? I thought you still had a couple of weeks' worth of work to do." She turned to face him, and Nikos felt a swift stab of fear go through him. "Hey. What's wrong?"

"Nikos, there's something I need to tell you. Something you need to know—"

A knock at the front door startled them both. Nikos raised one finger to Lexi. "Hold that thought, okay?"

But when he opened the front door, he found his Realtor, Cora Parish, standing there with a stack of folders in her arms. She smiled brightly at him. "I was in the neighborhood and thought I'd stop by to see how the staging went. I'd love to take a look at the room arrangements, if that's okay. I also brought some paperwork that we need to go over before the open house. Is now a good time?"

Pushing down his frustration, Nikos glanced at Lexi, but she gave a small wave of her hand and smiled. "It's okay, I'm pretty beat. I should probably go home and take a shower, and then make it an early night."

Before Nikos could protest that he wanted her to stay, she pushed past him, pausing only long enough to press a swift kiss against his cheek before she nodded to Cora and made her way down the front steps.

"I'll come by later," Nikos called to her, wishing he

could turn the Realtor away and go after Lexi. Something was up, and he had a sinking sense that it had nothing to do with his selling the house.

10

WHERE THE HELL WAS SHE? Nikos glanced at his watch for what seemed like the tenth time in less than an hour. Lexi knew the open house was tonight, so why wasn't she here? Already, dozens of guests milled through the rooms, eating and drinking and admiring his work. Waitstaff passed trays of appetizers and cocktails, and a wine-and-beer bar had been set up outside near the swimming pool. The event had been under way for less than an hour, but he'd expected Lexi long before now. In fact, he hadn't seen her at all since he'd left her bed that morning.

Stepping outside, he surveyed the backyard. The pergola and trees had been strung with twinkling lights. The underwater pool lights threw watery reflections over the patio, and in the distance, the city of Santa Barbara sparkled under the night sky. Nikos knew he should mingle with his guests and enjoy the fruits of his labor, but he found he couldn't relax or appreciate the success of the evening without Lexi there beside him. Glancing over at her house, he saw her windows were still dark. She hadn't returned home, and she wasn't answering her cell phone. Frustrated, he accepted a drink from a server and turned back to the house to see Cora walking toward him. She gave him a wide smile and looked around with approval.

"What did I tell you?" she asked as she joined him, lifting her own glass of white wine. "I'd say your open house is an overwhelming success. I counted nearly fifty people inside, and before long, your backyard is going to be overflowing, as well."

Nikos tapped his glass against hers. "I have you to thank. This was a great idea."

"I think I saw your Hollywood director inside. I wouldn't be surprised if he makes you an even better offer tonight."

Nikos nodded. "I spoke with him earlier. He did increase the amount, and I've decided to accept."

Cora paused with her glass halfway to her mouth. "What? But it's still early. You'll get half a dozen offers before the night is over. Why would you take the first one?"

Nikos shrugged. "I like the director, and I can actually picture him raising a family in this house."

Cora arched an eyebrow but didn't argue further. "I saw your girlfriend earlier tonight," she said, sipping her wine.

Nikos stilled. "Where was she?"

"There's an open house at a gallery downtown. I know the owner, so I stopped by for just a few minutes on my way here. I didn't actually speak with Lexi, but the owner said one of her sculptures is making its public debut tonight." She gave Nikos a conspiratorial wink. "I have to say, it's an amazing piece of work. She's extremely talented, but she obviously had some great inspiration."

Nikos frowned. Was it the sculpture she had been working so hard on over the past few months? And if it was, why hadn't she told him that she was showing it at a local gallery? Unless she didn't want to pull him away from his own event, which was ridiculous. There was no reason why they couldn't attend both together.

"I'm sorry," he said to Cora, "but I need to ask a favor of you."

Cora read his expression and her mouth opened on a protest. "Oh, no. You can't leave. These people are here to see your house. They'll be making offers, expecting you to talk to them about the restoration process!"

"You can tell them the house is already under agreement, and my cousins can speak to them about the work we did. I really have to go."

"But—"

He left her standing next to the swimming pool staring after him in dismay, but he didn't care. He'd left his truck at home that morning and had driven his sports car. He cut through the yard to Lexi's driveway where he had parked it. He knew exactly where the gallery was located, and with luck, he could be there in under twenty minutes.

LEXI STOOD INSIDE THE GALLERY, trying to be unobtrusive. She had dressed in a simple black cocktail dress for Nikos's open house and had been preparing to walk next door when the security company for her studio contacted her. Their alert system indicated that someone had gained access to the studio, but had neglected to enter the security code into the keypad. The result was that the alarm had been silently activated. Lexi wasn't worried and had declined the company's offer to send a security guard down to the studio to check it out. She was certain it was either a glitch in the system, or Nelda had decided at the last minute to use the studio to store some large pieces, in preparation for the gallery's black-tie event. She could reset the system and return to the open house before Nikos even missed her.

But she had been unprepared to walk into her studio and

find her sculpture of Apollo missing. On the rolling pedestal where he had once stood was a note that read, *"Please don't be upset. You'll thank me later. Nelda."*

Panicked, Lexi had raced to the gallery, appalled to find her sculpture the main attraction at Nelda's black-tie open house. Without exception, every person there was interested in just one thing: Apollo. He dominated the long, elegant studio, standing nearly eight feet tall as he regally surveyed the dozens of guests. His body gleamed beneath the studio lights, but it was the expression on his face that seemed to distance him, godlike, from his admirers. Lexi had perfectly captured Nikos's half smile, and just a hint of dimple showed in one lean cheek. On a small pedestal next to the sculpture, a placard read simply Apollo.

"He's amazing," one woman murmured, and dared to reach toward the sculpture. But her fingers hesitated over his corrugated abdomen, and finally, she dropped her hand. Lexi knew exactly how the woman felt. When something was that perfect, you almost didn't dare to touch it.

"Your sculpture is the star attraction," a voice murmured next to her, and Lexi turned to see a beaming Nelda. "I can't remember the last time the gallery had such a successful event."

Lexi stared at the other woman in disbelief. "How could you do this to me?"

"How could I *not?*" Glancing around them, she drew Lexi to one side. "Please don't be upset. You're such an amazing artist, and this sculpture deserves to be seen. To keep it locked up in your studio would be infinitely worse than what I did in bringing him here."

Lexi felt close to tears. "I want him returned to the studio first thing tomorrow morning. And I want my key back." She passed a hand over her eyes. "I can't believe you did this."

"Are you kidding?" Nelda said beneath her breath, smiling at a passing customer. "He's the main attraction! At least I didn't put your name on the card, although everyone wants to know who the artist is. Honestly, Lexi, I'm not sure how long I can keep you under wraps."

"Well, you need to, at least until I tell Nikos."

"Tell Nikos what?" asked a deep voice in her ear, and Lexi turned to see him standing beside her. As it always did, her heart leaped at the sight of him and a wave of heat washed through her, making her legs go a little weak. He looked good enough to eat in a white shirt that emphasized his tawny skin. He had rolled the sleeves back over his strong wrists, and pushed his hands casually into the pockets of his black dress pants.

"Nikos," she exclaimed, aware that Nelda's jaw had fallen open. She didn't blame her friend. Nikos in the flesh could be a little overwhelming. "How did you know I was here? Why aren't you at the house?"

"Cora Parish told me you were here. She said that one of your sculptures was on exhibit. You really think I would miss this debut?" His eyes gleamed warmly. "I know how hard you've worked over the past couple of months. I would never miss this."

Lexi's gaze flew guiltily toward the far end of the gallery where Apollo stood. Before she could say anything, Nikos turned to look in the same direction. As if someone had choreographed this moment, the spectators standing in front of the sculpture moved away, leaving both Nikos and Lexi with an unobstructed view of her work. Although he gave no outward indication, Lexi knew the precise instant that Nikos recognized the statue as himself.

"Is this your sculpture?" His voice was low.

"I can explain," Lexi began, but Nelda cut in.

"Bringing it here was my idea," she said quickly. "Just

look at the wonderful reception the piece is getting. I'm sure you can appreciate just how talented Lexi is. She was uncertain how you might feel about her having used you as her inspiration."

"*Used me* is an apt way of putting it," Nikos replied, shifting his attention to Lexi. "Do you mind if I take a closer look?"

Without waiting for her response, he made his way through the crowd to the pedestal where Apollo stood. He circled the statue as Lexi watched and she knew he missed nothing. But when he finally shifted his attention back to her, she was unprepared for his bleak expression. Without a word, he made his way out the door.

"Nikos, wait," Lexi said urgently, following him. "Please, try to understand. I'd almost finished the sculpture before you told me about your past. I didn't know. Nikos—"

He stopped on the sidewalk and spun toward her. "The day you came over to get your camera, you asked me to model for you. I refused. So *don't* tell me that you didn't know. You knew. You simply chose to disregard my feelings."

"Nikos, please—"

"Do you deny it? Can you stand there and tell me to my face that you honestly believed I would have no problem with you sculpting me *nude?*" He gave a disbelieving laugh. "If you'd done it solely for your own personal pleasure, that would be one thing, but to put me on display like this—" He bit the words off as two women walked past, eyeing them curiously, and entered the studio.

"I had no idea that sculpture would be here tonight. I was even having second thoughts about giving it to the botanic gardens. Please believe me," she said miserably. "I'm so sorry this happened."

"Yeah, me, too," he replied. "Sorry that I was so completely wrong about you. Enjoy the sculpture, because that's all you're getting of me. I hope it was worth whatever you're being paid for it."

Before Lexi could say another word, Nikos turned and walked away. She watched him leave, knowing it was futile to go after him. She'd seen his eyes. Like that first morning when he had retrieved her camera from the bushes, they were filled with both regret and disappointment. He wanted nothing to do with her.

Nelda came to stand beside her, and they watched as Nikos's sports car pulled away from the curb and roared off. "Give him a couple of days," her friend suggested. "He's upset now, but he'll come around."

"You're wrong," she said, her voice tight with suppressed emotion. "I don't think he will. I betrayed his trust. I knew he wouldn't approve of the sculpture, and yet I did it anyway. Worse, you brought it here and made it—made *him*—a spectacle."

"A sensation," Nelda corrected gently. "Tonight's exhibit made him a sensation."

"He won't forgive me for this," she said quietly. Nikos had refused to see his father for sixteen years. Lexi had no illusions that she was more important to him than his own parent.

Nelda laid a hand on her arm. "Then it's up to you to make him understand. I'm sorry, Lexi. I never meant for this to happen. I can see how you feel about him. Now you need to tell him."

LEXI SAT ON A LOW STOOL IN HER studio and stared moodily at her sculpture of Apollo.

Of Nikos.

He stood in the center of the cavernous space, his expression one of mild interest. His muscular body gleamed softly in the sunlight, and almost against her will, Lexi found herself approaching him. Reaching out, she laid her hand against his sculpted chest. The stone was cool and hard beneath her fingers. There was no heartbeat, no warmth, no sign of life. Glancing at his face, she saw that his expression hadn't changed. He continued to stare out across the studio, giving no indication that he knew—or even cared—that she was there.

Four days had passed since that horrible night at Studio Gallery, and she hadn't seen Nikos once. She knew the house next door had been sold because the staging company had come to remove the furniture and accessories and a sign had appeared on the front lawn that read Under Agreement.

But Nikos hadn't returned to the house.

Lexi had tried to contact him, but her calls went directly to his voice mail. Finally, she'd called his cousin, who had told her that Nikos had left for Syros the day after the open house, to visit his parents.

Drawing in a deep breath, Lexi let her hand fall away from the sculpture. As perfect as it was, she found the figure gave her no satisfaction. Instead, it taunted her, a beautifully cruel reminder of what she could have had. Had she really thought that all she wanted was a stone-cold statue? Had there actually been a time when she'd believed that a marble man was better than the flesh-and-blood deal? She knew now that the sculpture was nothing more than a poor imitation of what she really wanted.

Nikos.

He'd argued that he was far from perfect, but Lexi realized he was perfect for her. No other man could compare to him, not even her perfect marble creation.

It was then that she knew what she had to do.

"NIKOS, I NEED YOU."

Nikos straightened and turned from where he had been leaning on the railing of his parents' balcony, contemplating the waters of the Aegean. His mother stood just inside the double French doors, her green eyes unfathomable.

"What is it?" he asked.

"Come, I will show you."

He followed her through the house and into the living room. His father stood on the far side of the room speaking with a young woman, and for a heart-stopping instant Nikos thought he was hallucinating.

Lexi.

How many times during the past week had he fantasized about her being on Syros with him? As much as he enjoyed reconnecting with his family, he thought he'd go a little crazy with missing her. After the initial shock of seeing the sculpture had worn off, his anger and disappointment had dissipated quickly. In fact, from the moment he'd arrived on Syros, he'd regretted not staying to try to work things out. Instead, he'd convinced himself that a little bit of time and distance would give him some perspective. How many times would he let his own stubbornness and pride get in the way of being with those he loved?

Looking at Lexi now, he acknowledged that he did love her. He was crazy about her. Even reconciling with his father hadn't fully eased the ache of not being with her. She was looking at him now with a mixture of joy and apprehension that tugged at his heart.

"Lexi," he said, walking toward her. "I can't believe you're here."

Up close, he could see the signs of stress and fatigue on her face that had nothing to do with the long flight from California. She looked weary, as if she hadn't slept in days.

More than anything, he wanted to haul her into his arms and reassure her that everything would be okay.

"I had to come," she said simply, but Nikos heard the catch in her voice and knew she was close to losing it.

He turned to his parents to ask for some privacy, but they had slipped silently from the room, leaving him alone with Lexi.

"First, let me apologize for the sculpture," she said hurriedly, as if she was afraid he might toss her out before she'd had her say. "When I first saw you, I couldn't believe how beautiful you were. That day we had lunch on your patio, I knew I wanted to create Apollo in your image. I never meant to offend you, and by the time I guessed how you might feel, it was too late."

"Stop." He interrupted her frantic flow of words to drag her into his arms. "I'm the one who should apologize, not you."

She stared at him, clearly bemused. "What?"

He smiled into her eyes, but his voice was serious. "I overreacted that night at the gallery. Instead of being insulted, I should have felt honored. And I do. I'm humbled, really, both by your talent and your portrayal of Apollo."

Lexi smoothed her fingers over the front of his shirt. "I'm half-afraid that you're just being nice. But I am sorry," she said softly. "When I first met you, all I could think about was sculpting you. Then I got so caught up in capturing your image that I forgot about what mattered. You. Us."

"Is that why you're here?"

She raised her eyes to his. "Yes. The sculpture is perfect, Nikos, but it isn't you."

He gave her a half smile and smoothed her hair back with one finger. "You're right. I'm not perfect. Not even close."

"I'm not giving the sculpture to the botanic gardens. It will stay in my studio."

"Are you sure? Because I've been doing a lot of thinking since I've been here, and I think it should be placed in the gardens."

"You do?"

"Absolutely. You put so much of yourself into that statue, it would be a shame to keep it locked away somewhere." Nikos gave a soft laugh. "I think I was actually a little jealous of Apollo, and how much time you spent working on him."

Lexi winced. "When I first met you, I was a little down on relationships. I thought that I could get involved with you without falling in love with you. I really believed that all I wanted was to create a sculpture of the perfect man." She gave a soft, self-deprecating laugh. "And now that I have it, I find he's not what I want at all."

Nikos used his knuckles to smooth her hair away from her face. "What do you want?"

"You, Nikos. Only you. With all your imperfections, if they really exist."

Slowly, Nikos raised her hand to his mouth. "Oh, they exist," he assured her softly. "It only took me eighteen years to return to Syros and make peace with my father. I'm proud and stubborn, and that's just the beginning."

Lexi wound her arms tighter around him. "I don't care. If you lost your looks tomorrow and all that remained was your pride and stubbornness, I would still want you. You see, to me you're perfect."

Nikos groaned and buried his face in her hair. "I was angry that night because I'd fallen for you, and I couldn't stand to think you might have only been interested in me as a model."

"Maybe that's how it began," she said, "but that's not

how I feel now. I don't care about the sculpture, Nikos. Not anymore."

"I have to warn you that I'm not perfect. And you shouldn't want me to be."

"Why not?"

"Because being perfect means never losing control, and I've found that where you're concerned, I have very little control."

"I'm glad," Lexi murmured, and leaned toward him, her gaze fixed on his mouth.

Nikos gave a soft groan, and cupping the back of her head in his hand, covered her lips with his. There was nothing tentative or apologetic about the kiss; it was deep and possessive, and when Lexi moved closer, he reveled in the feel of her beneath his hands.

"Christ, I've missed you," he muttered against her mouth. Pulling slightly back, he studied her face. "I'll make you a deal. In the future, I'll model for you anytime you want, so long as the finished product is for your eyes only."

Lexi nodded, her eyes shining. "It's a deal."

A discreet cough came from the kitchen, and Nikos gave her a grin. "Would you like to meet the rest of my family? Because unless I'm mistaken, my mother will have spread the word that you're here. I have no doubt that my brothers and sisters are all congregated in the next room, dying to meet you."

Lexi swallowed, looking a little panicky. "Okay. If you're sure."

"Oh, I am. And then tomorrow, we'll leave here and spend a week on the island of Santorini."

Her eyes widened. "Nikos! How—"

"I made the reservations weeks ago, before the open house."

"But how did you know that I would follow you here? Is that why you didn't cancel them?"

Nikos caught her face between his hands. "Let's just say that I hoped you would come," he murmured. "I find that I have a lot of hope for our future…a perfect future."

He kissed her slowly.

Thoroughly.

Completely.

* * * * *

COMING NEXT MONTH from Harlequin® Blaze™

AVAILABLE OCTOBER 16, 2012

#717 THE PROFESSIONAL

Men Out of Uniform

Rhonda Nelson

Jeb Anderson might look like an angel, but he's a smooth-tongued devil with a body built for sin. Lucky for massage therapist Sophie O'Brien, she knows just what to do with a body like that....

#718 DISTINGUISHED SERVICE

Uniformly Hot!

Tori Carrington

It's impossible to live in a military town without knowing there are few things sexier than a man in uniform. Geneva Davis believes herself immune...until hotter than hot Marine Mace Harrison proves that a military man *out* of uniform is downright irresistible.

#719 THE MIGHTY QUINNS: RONAN

The Mighty Quinns

Kate Hoffmann

When Ronan Quinn arrives in Sibleyville, Maine, he finds not just a job, but an old curse, a determined matchmaker and a beautiful woman named Charlie. But is earth-shattering sex enough to convince him to give up the life he's built in Seattle?

#720 YOURS FOR THE NIGHT

The Berringers

Samantha Hunter

P.I. in training Tiffany Walker falls head-over-heels in lust for her mentor, sexy Garrett Berringer. But has she really found the perfect job *and* the perfect man?

#721 A KISS IN THE DARK

The Wrong Bed

Karen Foley

Undercover agent Cole MacKinnon hasn't time for a hookup until he rescues delectable Lacey Delaney after her car breaks down. But how can he risk his mission—even to keep the best sex of his life?

#722 WINNING MOVES

Stepping Up

Lisa Renee Jones

Jason Alright and Kat Moore were young and in love once, but their careers tore them apart. Now, fate has thrown them together again and given them one last chance at forever. But can they take it?

Bestselling Harlequin® Blaze™ author Rhonda Nelson is back with yet another irresistible Man out of Uniform. Meet Jebb Willington—former ranger, current security agent and all-around good guy. His assignment—to catch a thief at an upscale retirement residence. The problem—he's falling for sexy massage therapist Sophie O'Brien, the woman he's trying to put behind bars....

Read on for a sneak peek at THE PROFESSIONAL

Available November 2012 only from Harlequin Blaze.

Oh, hell.

Former ranger Jeb Willingham didn't need extensive army training to recognize the telltale sound that emerged roughly ten feet behind him. He was Southern, after all, and any born-and-bred Georgia boy worth his salt would recognize the distinct metallic click of a 12-gauge shotgun. And given the decided assuredness of the action, he knew whoever had him in their sights was familiar with the gun and, more important, knew how to use it.

"On your feet, hands where I can see them," she ordered. He had to hand it to her. Sophie O'Brien was cool as a cucumber. Her voice was steady, not betraying the slightest bit of fear. Which, irrationally, irritated him. He was a strange man trespassing on her property—she ought to be afraid, dammit. Why hadn't she stayed in the house and called 911 like a normal woman?

Oh, right, he thought sarcastically. Because she wasn't a *normal* woman. She was kind and confident, fiendishly clever and sexy as hell.

He wanted her.

HBEXP1112

And the hell of it? Aside from the conflict of interest and the tiny matter of *her name at the top of his suspect list?*

She didn't like him.

"Move," she said again, her voice firmer. "I'd rather not shoot you, but I will if you don't stand up and turn around."

Beautiful, Jeb thought, feeling extraordinarily stupid. He'd been an army ranger, one of the fiercest soldiers among Uncle Sam's finest...and he'd been bested by a massage therapist with an Annie Oakley complex.

With a sigh, he got up and flashed a grin at her. "Evening, Sophie. Your shrubs need mulching."

She gasped, betraying the first bit of surprise. It was ridiculous how much that pleased him. "You?" she breathed. "What the hell are you doing out here?"

He pasted a reassuring look on his face and gestured to the gun still aimed at his chest. "Would you mind lowering your weapon? It's a bit unnerving."

She brought the barrel down until it was aimed directly at his groin. "There," she said, a smirk in her voice. "Feel better?"

Has Jebb finally met his match? Find out in
THE PROFESSIONAL

Available November 2012
wherever Harlequin Blaze books are sold.

HBEXP1112